What It's All About

On the plane going home Suzu made a fuss again. She said the lady on the other plane said she could fly the plane herself on the way back. So all the stewardesses were running around trying to make her happy and giving her special magazines and straws.

When she was back there playing with them, I said to Mom, "Are you sorry we adopted Suzu?"

"No, why should I be sorry?"

"Well, you said to Peggy how much easier it would be without children."

"Hon, listen," Mom said. "Sometimes, of course I feel that way. Just like you sometimes feel life would be easier without me. But most of the time I feel that without the two of you life wouldn't be worth a hang. Having things easy isn't what it's all about."

NORMA KLEIN

What It's All About

AN ARCHWAY PAPERBACK
POCKET BOOKS . NEW YORK

To Herb, Judy, Antonia, Erica
and Joshua Kohl

Contents

Waiting for Suzu   1
The Airport   11
Nice and Not So Nice   21
A Visit from Grandma   30
Honey, Ya Can't Love One   41
Going to Boston   48
Dad and Peggy Get Married   56
The Bridesmaid Returns Home   66
Grandma Meets a Lovely Widower   72
Fooling Mrs. Mondale   77
Christmas at Jonah's   87
Secrets   99
Funny Business   107
A Telegram from Dad   111
What's Your Bag?   119
Baby Weekend   129
Francesca   135
The Christmas Party   143

What It's All About

Waiting for Suzu

"How come she's bald?" Jonah asked. "I thought she was three or something."

"I think they had to shave her head," I said, looking at the photo with him. "Maybe she had lice or something."

Jonah made a face. "Boy, I hope she doesn't have them when you get her."

"No, she'll be O.K."

"When're you getting her?"

"In a couple of weeks, probably. They write and let you know first."

Of course, Jonah doesn't think it's so exciting to be getting a younger child in the family because he has one in his already—his brother, Zachary, who's four and a half. Zachary really loves Jonah a lot. If he's invited to a birthday party, even, he won't go unless Jonah goes with him. I don't know if Suzu will be like that with me because I'm not her real sister; that might make a difference.

"I'm going to have to teach her English," I said.

"Doesn't she know any?"

"Uh uh. They just found her in South Vietnam, kind of wandering around the streets. Mom says they call them street children because that's where they live—in the streets. They have to beg and stuff like that."

"What happened to her mother and father?"

"Her mother might've died, Mom said. And her father might have been an American soldier because she looks a little bit American."

"What happened to him?"

"I guess he went home . . . or maybe he was shot or something."

In the beginning, when Mom said we were going to adopt a Vietnamese child, I was really excited. In fact, I used to think about it all the time. But then it began taking so long! I was nine when Mom went over for this TV program and now I'm eleven. The thing is, Mom said that even though she knew she wanted Suzu, there are just lots of delays you can't do anything about. She said you simply have to be patient. I have been patient, but now that it's finally about to happen, it's hard to believe it's real. We fixed up Suzu's room about nine months ago and it's just sort of sitting there. Sometimes I go into it and sit on the bed to make the room know we haven't forgotten and that someone will really live there. But if I was that room, I think I might wonder.

Jonah and I go to this private school in New York called The Whitman School. It's right near where I live, so on nice days I can even walk home. I live on Ninety-sixth Street between Central Park West and Columbus. We have part of a brownstone, and the rest has other people in it. When Jonah comes to visit me after school, we always walk up Columbus so we can stop at Mr. Clark's stationery store. We get Wacky Packs or candy or stuff like that. What's not fair is that Jonah not only gets an allowance, but his mother gives him a dime for every book he reads to Zachary, so he has the sixth series and most of the seventh. We used to trade Wacky Packs at school, but our fifth-grade teacher, Mrs. Salas, said we were wasting too much time and we couldn't bring them in anymore. So Jonah and me only get to trade them after school.

"Most people adopt babies who are *real* babies," Jonah said.

"Well, Mom said she didn't want to go through the whole baby thing again. Anyway, she says these children need homes more because no one wants them once they're big."

One thing I don't understand is why we had to get a girl. We have a girl already—me—so why not get a boy? It would have been nice to get a boy my age like Jonah. Then we could've all played together. But Mom says when she saw Suzu, something about her just appealed to her. There was a kind of gleam in her eye, she said, even though she'd had such a hard life. Mom is sort of crazy about kids. She's a newscaster for an educational channel and lots of her TV programs are about kids doing things. She says kids are more honest about what they say.

At Mr. Clark's we each got five new packs. You have to check because sometimes they don't have all the ones they're supposed to. I got Swiss Mess Cocoa Mix. Jonah got Monotony. He has one of those already, but he can make a double by pasting them together back to back, so that's not so bad. That way you can trade it for two new ones.

"I got Clammy Soap," Jonah said, shuffling through his.

"Darn, you're always getting the good ones."

"What'd you get?"

I showed him mine. Creature Crackers, Graft Cheese, Super Cigar Crisp, Snarlamint Cigarettes, and Fruit of the Tomb T-shirts.

"I think I might get a Mars Bar," Jonah said thoughtfully. "I still have fifteen cents."

Jonah's not supposed to eat candy between meals. He's not fat really, just a little plump, but his mother thinks he should lose weight because she thinks then he'd be better at sports. Jonah says he just doesn't like sports and it has nothing

4

to do with being plump, but she doesn't believe him.

"Can I have a bite?" I said. I really don't like Mars Bars so much, but if I eat some, then Jonah won't get so fat. He let me take a bite, but he watched me so I couldn't take much.

We went back to my house. Nobody was home yet because Mom works late on Tuesday, and Gabe, my stepfather, is usually at his studio. He teaches art, but his real thing is making sculptures. He makes them out of automobile bumpers.

My room is on the second floor and so is the room Suzu will have. We have three floors. At the very top is Mom and Gabe's bedroom and another room which is sort of a study. It has this old typewriter in it that Mom bought when she was in college. She gave it to me. I'm going to be a writer when I grow up. Really I am one right now, but I haven't published anything yet. I want to send my stories in to places, but Mom says I'm too young. I don't see why I can't. I wouldn't have to tell them how old I was. Mom says they could tell anyway. I don't see how. I spell really well and everything. She says there's time enough for all that and I should enjoy being a child. Grown-ups always say that.

Jonah likes to sit near my bedroom window and look out. I have these binoculars and he likes to look at people going down the street. Sometimes we play we're spies and those people are people we have to watch because we know they're going to steal enemy secrets.

"Hey, Bern!" That's Gabe. He usually comes home at four.

"What?" I yelled down.

"Did you get the envelopes?"

"I forgot!"

"Listen, babes, I reminded you twice."

Jonah looked at me. "Let's go get them, then."

"Why can't he get his own stupid envelopes?" I said.

"My mother makes me get things sometimes too," Jonah said. He always tries to make me feel better. "Why don't you walk me home and you can get them on the way back?"

"O.K., let's go." I need some Scotch tape for this report I'm doing for school, so it won't be a complete waste.

Jonah lives on Eighty-sixth between Central Park West and Columbus so I stopped at Mr. Clark's again. I guess I was so busy with the Wackies that I forgot the first time. When I got home, Gabe was sitting in the sling chair, drinking some beer. "Here," I said, throwing the envelopes at him real quick. He caught it in one hand. He has pretty quick reflexes. Gabe's tall and heavy and has curly brown hair. You should see him in a bathing suit. He has hair all *over* his shoulders and legs and everything. I guess that's supposed to be sexy or something.

"Thanks, Bernadette, sweetheart," Gabe said.

6

He knows I hate being called Bernadette. It's my name, but mostly people call me Bernie or Bern. Bernadette is yucky. I hate it. I don't know how Mom could have thought up such a yucky name. She says that it wasn't her choice, it was Dad's. By Dad I mean my real father, Fumio. He's Japanese. Really, he's Japanese-American since he was born in America, in Chicago actually. Now he lives in San Francisco. He's an architect and he has this really great house which is a dome. I love it. When I was nine, I visited him for Christmas. I flew out with a friend of Mom's who was taking her vacation there. I wish I could go more, but Mom says it's too expensive. So usually I just see him when he comes East on business trips, which is not too often, just once or twice a year. Gabe is O.K., but I definitely don't like him as much as Dad, and if you ask my opinion, Mom should never have gotten a divorce. But no one ever did ask my opinion. Maybe that was because I was only four when it happened.

There was some time before supper so I went up to the study to type. If I can't think of a name for a character in a story I'm writing, I pick one out of the *Name Your Baby Book*. That has regular names like Mary and Jonathan. I also have this one called *The New Age Baby Name Book*, which has really far-out names like Yunus and Ragnar. I got Suzu out of *The New Age Baby Name Book*. Mom said I could pick the name. She said it was up to me, but she thought an

7

Oriental name would be nice. Actually, Suzu is Japanese, but her middle name, Tran Thi, is her own Vietnamese name. Mom thought Suzu sounded more American and would be easier for people to say. Mom said she would have liked me to have a Japanese name too, but Dad for some crazy reason just loved the name Bernadette! My middle name, Chika, is Japanese. One reason Mom wanted to adopt a Vietnamese child was so we both would have an Oriental heritage. She says when I'm older, maybe I can visit Japan and China with Dad so I'll know more about it. I never even met my Japanese grandma and grandpa because when I was born, they had died already.

I really love looking up names in the *Name Your Baby Book*. Sometimes I just sit there reading it like it was a real book. It tells things like what the name means. Bernadette means "brave as a bear." Actually, I don't know if that's a good name for me because I'm not all that brave. I used to even sleep with a light on in my room till I was eight.

Suzu means "little bell." In the book it says they put this bell in a "silk charm purse" and "attach it to a child's girdle so that whenever she moves, a pretty tinkling is heard." I'm not sure what a silk charm purse is. I guess it must be like a ladies' pocketbook. But I don't know why a child would have one. I also can't figure out why a child would wear a girdle unless she was very fat. I wouldn't want to have our Suzu wear a bell; it would be too noisy. Of course, in Japan it's probably different. The book says "originally it was thought the sound would frighten demons." Since we don't have demons, that wouldn't be a problem. It also says it was believed it "would keep the child from falling." I don't see how a bell could keep a child from falling! They must figure it's magic. Anyhow, I really picked Suzu because of the way it sounds. Even if she has a nickname, it'll be "Su," which is pretty, not "Bern" or "Bernie" so that no one can even tell if you're a boy or a girl!

At seven when I was downstairs setting the table, Mom came into the kitchen. "Mom, did you know in Japan little children wear girdles?"

But Mom didn't look like she heard me. She was waving this envelope in the air. "Bernie! She's coming! Monday!"

"This Monday?"

"Yes! In six days. Wow, can you believe it? Finally!"

I ran upstairs to look at Suzu's room. I had put these dolls on her bed that I don't play with anymore. "Get set, kids!" I told them. "The big day is coming."

They just sat there. Well, what do you expect with dolls? I hope Suzu won't mind that they don't work anymore. You can still do regular things with them like give them a bath or get them dressed. But they don't do special things anymore like tell you what time it is or talk if you pull their string.

After supper I think I'll make a sign saying Welcome Suzu to put on her door. I could put Welcome Home, Suzu, but I think you can only do that if the person is coming back to a place where they've already been. Just plain Welcome is the best. Of course, she can't read English, but it's the thought that counts. That's what they always say.

The Airport

Today Suzu came to our family.

We all waited at the airport. It was a school day, but Mom said I could miss it because it was a special occasion. She was sort of dressed up in a long flowered skirt and a black turtleneck. Mom is tall and thin and she has curly brown hair. People say I look like her, but I think that's just because I'm tall and thin too. Really, I look like Dad, my eyes and hair anyway. I tried not to act too excited. When the people from the adoption agency came to our house, Mom said I should act natural, but very nice. It's hard to act natural *and* very nice. What if you're in a bad mood? But Mom said because she and Gabe had both been divorced, they might think Suzu was coming to an unsettled home.

"Mom, when are they coming? I thought it was supposed to be twelve."

"There must be a delay because of the weather," Mom said.

"I hope the plane doesn't crash," I said.

"Hon, come on!"

"Aren't you nervous, though?"

"Sure, but not about that."

For Mom I guess this is like giving birth to a baby, since she'll go home with a child the way you do when you come out of the hospital. I went over and sat down next to her, leaning on her. "Tell me about the night I was born," I said.

"Oh, God," Gabe said.

"Why shouldn't I tell her?" Mom said, turning to him.

"Go right ahead. I just think I've heard this particular saga about eight hundred times."

"You have *not*," I said, frowning.

Gabe got up and stretched. "I'm going to the men's room," he said and walked off.

"Why is he so sarcastic?" I said, hugging Mom.

"Hon, he's nervous."

"About Suzu?"

"Sure . . . he just doesn't like to admit it. It's a big thing for parents to be getting a new child."

"I bet he wishes it was a boy."

"No, he doesn't. He likes girls."

"He likes Francesca."

Francesca is Gabe's daughter from his first marriage. You see, it's sort of complicated. First

12

he got married at twenty-two to this girl from the town he grew up in called Munth (that's the town in Iowa; the girl's name I forget, but she was Prom Queen in his high school and Mom always just calls her P.Q. for short). He and P.Q. split up after six years and then awhile after that he met Mom, who was already divorced from Dad. The one and only time I met Francesca was two years ago, on May 20th, 1972, which is when Mom and Gabe got married. She didn't even stay over, just flew back the same day. Gabe keeps saying that one day, if P.Q. will agree, he would like Francesca to come and spend the summer with us so we can get to know each other. I really hope that happens. It would be great. She's practically my age, just six months older. I know Gabe does like her more than me, even if Mom says he doesn't. I guess he has to because she's his real daughter. Well, I like Dad a lot better than him, so I suppose we're even. But that's because Dad is a lot nicer, not just because he's my real father. Dad is never sarcastic or anything; he's an extremely kind person.

Mom was smiling. She's told me this story millions of times, but I still like to hear it. "The night you were born, it was absolutely pouring rain," Mom said. She always starts out like that.

"Tell the part about Grandma."

"Well, Grandma was going to come over after supper that night. It was Christmas day, but you weren't supposed to be born till January third,

13

so I figured I had a week or so more to go. Everybody'd told me first children are usually late, anyway."

"Were you excited though?"

"Fantastically. But I felt all ready; I had everything packed for the hospital. I wasn't scared, just excited. So Dad and I ate in, just some cold chicken. I wasn't that hungry. Then I noticed we were out of sugar and Grandma always likes sugar in her coffee, at least two spoons. So I went down the hall to borrow some from this neighbor of ours named June Ponticorvo."

"Was she surprised to see you?"

"Yes, she thought for some reason I'd already gone to the hospital, I guess because she hadn't seen me for a while. But she went in to get the sugar and while I was standing there this funny thing happened. My pants got all wet. I thought I was peeing in my pants!"

"You must have been so embarrassed!"

"I was! It was awful. I said to her, 'June, listen, I think I peed in my pants.' And she said—she had two kids of her own—she said, 'Oh, no, your bag of water must have broken. You're in labor.' "

"Didn't you know about that, that bag, from that course you took?"

"Yeah, only you learn so many things, Bern, you can't remember all of them. At least I couldn't. So, anyway, as soon as she said, 'You're in labor' I suddenly realized I had this awful pain in my stomach and they called the doctor and he said, 'Come to the hospital right away!' "

"You were all packed and ready, though."

"Right . . . only I hadn't expected the doctor would say come right away. I thought you were supposed to stay at home a long time. Usually it takes fifteen hours or so for a first baby."

"But I couldn't wait, I guess."

"No, you were sure in a hurry. You came out in three hours from the time I stood there asking June Ponticorvo for some sugar."

"Did it hurt?"

"It did, honey. It really hurt like hell. Which was funny because I'd been practicing these exercises and they said if you did them, you wouldn't feel a thing. I guess I'm a coward. Because when I got to the hospital and they asked, 'Do you want a shot?' I yelled, 'Yes, give me everything you've got!' "

"Weren't you scared of getting a shot?"

"No, it's funny. I never minded shots. So they stuck me with something, I forget what, and I fell asleep and then I was waking up and they were waving you at me and then they took you away before I'd even seen you really."

"Did you ask for me back?"

"Did I? I yelled and hollered. I said, 'You give me that baby back!' They said, 'No, madam, you can't see her yet. We have to clean her up.' I was so mad! They practically had to hold me down on the table."

"But then they brought me?"

"Finally . . . it seemed like about a million years later, they wheeled me to this room and tucked me in bed. I felt wide awake, even though it was two in the morning. 'Here she is,' they said and handed you to me."

"Was I cute?"

"You were funny. You had all this black hair, really a lot, enough to tie a ribbon on. It made you look so much cuter than all the other babies. I had thought I'd think you were really ugly because I never liked newborn babies, but I didn't. You looked really special."

I don't think I looked that special or cute, even if I did have all that hair. I saw this picture of me they took in the hospital and I looked really mad and scrunched up. But I guess mothers always think *their* babies are different.

"There it is! It's landing!" someone yelled.

We weren't the only people waiting to pick up a child. There were several other families. My heart started beating really fast. Mom took my hand and we went right over to the window so we could see them getting off the plane.

"That's her!" I whispered. I could tell from the photo. All her hair had grown in. She was coming down this ramp, holding the hand of another little girl. The other little girl looked about a year younger. They were both wearing blue dresses. A lady came down carrying a baby.

Another lady came off the plane and she

started to try and separate Suzu from the other little girl. Suzu didn't mind, but the other little girl began to yell and scream. I felt so sorry for her. "Is that her sister?" I asked. I thought maybe we should adopt both of them.

"No, it must be a friend or something," Mom said.

A few minutes later a door opened and Suzu walked over to us. The woman with her said, "Is Mrs. Sobel here?"

Mom nodded. "This must be Suzu."

Suzu was standing there, really solemnly. She didn't seem upset like that other little girl. She didn't smile. She just looked at us. It must be strange to come to a place where everybody speaks a language you don't know. I mean, if you're a baby I guess it's easier because you don't know any language so you don't care. But it was funny to think she must be thinking things that she couldn't tell us about.

"Hi, Suzu," I said. They said they had told her her new name a few months ago so she'd get used to it.

Mom took one of her hands and I took one and we walked out to the car. Gabe had gone ahead to bring the car to where we were.

She was really quiet on the way home. So were we. I guess we couldn't think of what to say, especially since she didn't know English. Mom said she'd pick it up listening to us.

17

After we got out of the car, Gabe said, "O.K., I'll see you later, folks."

Mom whirled around and glared at him. "What do you mean? Where are you going?"

"To the studio—look, sweetheart, I'm swamped with work. I'm supposed to get that show together pretty soon, remember? I can't afford to just waste a whole day—"

"Waste!"

Gabe sighed. "Becka, don't be uptight, O.K.? We have her, she's great, don't make a whole big song and dance. I'll be back for dinner. See you then."

After he left Mom just stood there. She still had that mad expression on her face.

"I took the day off from school," I said.

"I know, hon, I'm glad you did too. Well, let's see, how about a little snack? Would you like something to eat, Suzu?" To me she said, "Just talk in a regular way, even if she can't understand. She'll pick it up very fast, just watch."

Mom brought out some cake and ham and other things. "You don't have to eat it if you don't want to, Suzu," she said. "Just eat it if you feel like it."

I guess Suzu was hungry because she sat down and gobbled up everything on her plate. She didn't use a spoon or fork or anything.

"She isn't used to silverware," Mom said. "Remember, it's going to take her awhile to get used to all these new things."

18

After the snack we showed Suzu her room. It's next to mine. The dolls were still sitting there on the bed and my "Welcome Suzu" sign was right over their heads. "This is where you'll sleep, Suzu," Mom said, "and these are your toys."

But Suzu seemed more interested in the wallpaper, which showed a bear hanging onto a bunch of colored balloons. Very carefully she touched the balloons.

"Those are balloons," I said. "Hey, Mom, I have a great idea. I have these balloons left over from Jonah's party. Maybe she'd like it if I blew some up for her."

"Great. I'll get some string."

Suzu followed me into my room. I decided to do what Mom said, just talk like she understood me. "See, Jonah had this party," I said, "and we got to take home some stuff." I got out the balloons. "They're just like the wallpaper in your room, only I've got to blow them up. You watch."

Suzu watched while I blew up the balloons. Then I tied them with string and gave them to her. Her eyes opened really wide. She just stood there, holding them. All the rest of the afternoon she carried them around everywhere.

"I guess she never saw balloons before," I told Mom.

"There're lots of things she's never seen," Mom said.

That night we tied the balloons onto the post

of Suzu's bed. If we let her sleep with them, she would roll over and burst them. But she might not know about that if she's never been to birthday parties.

So now I have a four-year-old sister. It makes me feel old in a way, being with a little child who doesn't know that much. I think if I teach her, she'll get good. You can tell by her face that she's a pretty smart kid. I think maybe she's smarter than Zachary, but I won't tell Jonah that because he might be jealous.

Nice and Not So Nice

"You know, your mother is really mean," I said to Jonah.

"Well, she thinks it will be good for me," he said. I could tell he really agreed with me. Jonah's mother is making him go back for the *second* time to this dumb camp in Maine where you do lots of active things. The idea is he'll lose weight, but the thing is he went one time and didn't lose weight at all. And nothing will be different this time, I just know.

Mom said I could go to camp if I wanted. I decided I don't want to. If I go to the kind of camp where you sleep away all summer, then I'll hardly see Suzu at all. And I don't like that other kind out of the city where you have to spend hours on this really hot bus singing camp songs.

I did that a couple of summers and I got really carsick. Anyhow, we have a yard to our brownstone and I can do stuff out there and take Suzu places. This Barnard girl, Cynthia, is coming during the day to look after Suzu, and she seems fairly nice. She's going to be a rabbi, she said. That's sort of interesting. I never met a religious Jewish person before. I'm half Jewish, from Mom, but we never do anything special about it like go to synagogue or anything.

"Maybe if you really do lose weight this summer, she won't make you go back again," I said hopefully.

"Yeah, but they give you all these things like marshmallows in your cocoa. It's not so easy," he said glumly.

"Anyway, why'd she pick a place so many miles away? I could come visit you if you were closer."

"I know . . . it's really lousy," he said.

"I'll write you," I said.

"I probably won't write back," Jonah admitted.

"Oh, I know," I said. "You didn't last year either. I like writing letters."

"That's good," he said. "I wish I did."

Jonah left on June twenty-eighth and I do miss him, but I think it's not going to be as bad as last summer because of Suzu. There are lots of things about Suzu that are different than you'd expect. Like I don't think she ever had baths that much before because she seems to think they're this great thing. I think she'd stay in the bath all day if you didn't make her get out. She just sits there and laughs and splashes around in the water. I have to wash her because she doesn't know how.

Sometimes she gets really mad and starts to scream. Mom says I have to understand that it's not just because she's from Vietnam and they do things differently there. She says it's that she never really lived in a real home with a mother and father. For a while she just roamed the streets with other kids before they found her and put her in the orphanage. So things anyone would know about, she doesn't. She doesn't seem to like sleeping in a bed or at least sometimes she just goes to sleep on the floor, without a blanket or a quilt or anything.

What I don't like is when she screams. Mom says she may just be mad that we don't understand her, and how would I like to come to a place where no one understood a word I said. Also, Suzu will sort of hoard things up in her room, like food. Mom found all these old pieces of meat under her bed in a bag. That must be because she doesn't know if she'll keep getting meat, so she wants to save it.

Once Mom had some friends over and when she was out of the room, Suzu begged from them. She wasn't ashamed or anything. I guess she thought that's what you should do. She just went right into the kitchen and put the money down on the table with a big smile, like she thought Mom would be proud of her.

One good thing is Suzu is starting to use English words for things. At first I couldn't understand her at all. You know what she calls me? "Nice." She comes over and yanks on my sleeve and says, "Nice—play." Only she doesn't seem to like the dolls I gave her that much. What she loves are these bean-bag frogs. When I make them stand on their heads, she laughs and laughs. It's pretty when she laughs, like a bell. I guess Suzu is a good name for her.

At night sometimes Suzu comes into my room. I'll wake up and there she is, sleeping on the floor, next to my bed.

"I think she must be used to sleeping with other people," Mom said. "Maybe she should go in with you for a while, Bern."

"But what if she likes it and wants to do it for the rest of her life?"

"She won't, don't worry."

"She could sleep in *your* room."

"No, she couldn't, hon. Don't be stubborn."

When I wake up in the morning, there she is, sitting there staring at me. I have a trundle bed where you pull out the bottom part—that's where Suzu sleeps. She sits right on her bed, cross-legged, looking at my face with these big black eyes. It makes me nervous because maybe she's been sitting there for three hours or something when I was asleep and I didn't even know it. "Nice up," she says when I open my eyes.

Before we got Suzu, I'd sometimes wake up early, but I'd lie in bed and read or something. Now, as soon as I wake up, she wants me to do stuff with her, like with the bean-bag frogs. I hoped Mom would give me a dime for every book I read to her, but she said No.

"Jonah's mother does," I said.

"The hell with Jonah's mother. It's corrupt and revolting."

"No, it's not . . . it's good for kids. It helps them learn."

"Then do it for the pleasure of it, not for the money."

"But you need an economic incentive," I said. I'm not sure what that means. It's an expression Jonah learned from his father.

"Hon, what the heck do you *need* with money, anyhow? You have money."

"I only have fourteen dollars and eighty cents," I said. "Some kids in our class have forty dollars!"

"Wow!"

"You don't even appreciate all the good things I do. I mean, it's not so great if you're eleven years old to have a little child sleeping in your room and waking you up first thing."

"Does she really wake you up?"

"Well, no . . . but she sits there watching me."

"You have a hard life, Bern, I mean it."

"You don't have to be so sarcastic."

"Honey!"

"Everybody in this house hates me."

"I don't. I love you."

"You just say that."

"Suzu does. She learned a name for you right off."

It's true, having Suzu is good. I like showing her things and teaching her. Maybe I can't really appreciate it so much because ever since we got her, things have been really bad around here. Gabe and Mom keep having these really terrible fights. It's not that I eavesdrop on them. They just talk so loud I can hear them whether I want to or not. Last night after Suzu went to sleep, they really had a whopper.

Gabe started in saying the house was always noisy from the little children Mom invites for Suzu.

Mom said he should go to his studio if the noise bothered him.

Gabe said why should he be driven from his own house?

Mom said it wasn't a matter of being driven. But it was important for Suzu to get to know other children and once her (Mom's) vacation was over, she wouldn't have so much time to arrange things like that.

Gabe said this was some vacation. He said he didn't see why they couldn't go off together and

26

leave the kids (meaning me too, I guess) with M and G. (Gabe calls Grandma, who is Mom's mother, Moaner and Groaner. I don't think that's so nice.)

Mom said she wanted to get Suzu really settled in. Maybe then they could go away for a weekend or something.

Gabe said a weekend was not his idea of a vacation.

Mom said why did he agree to adopt Suzu if he wasn't willing to give time to her the way she needed.

Gabe said it hadn't been him. She was the one who had the thing about adopting. She'd decided to adopt even before she met him and once she had that idea in her head, she wouldn't go back on it for anything. She was the one, he said, who wanted to save the world and give shelter to every unwanted creature that crawled the face of the earth.

Mom said she did *not* want to give shelter to every single creature. But she felt she had a responsibility to—

Right in the middle of that sentence Gabe yelled, "Listen, save that crap about saving the world for your job, will you?" And then I heard a big slam like he had walked out of the house.

I got up and went down to the kitchen. Mom was sitting at the table.

"How come Gabe's in such a bad mood?" I

said. I thought Mom might get mad at me for being up, but she just sighed and said, "Oh, Bern, it's complicated."

I nodded. I got some raisins and oatmeal cookies out. I was feeling quite hungry.

"Poor little Suzu," Mom said, sighing. "I wanted her to have such a happy start with us."

"She doesn't know."

"Oh, children know everything. They're supersensitive."

"They are?"

"Absolutely. They see, hear, and sense everything. You notice I'm not asking how come you heard our argument because what does it matter. You weren't standing there with your nose pressed to the door, I bet. You just heard."

"I think Suzu is happy here," I said. I got out some milk too. I can get very hungry at night. "She likes the baths and the bean-bag frogs."

"Sure," Mom said, sort of sadly. "You're probably right, Bern."

"Did Gabe really not want her? You said he liked little girls."

"Oh, I think he did want her. But maybe I pushed too hard because it meant so much to me. That was my fault. I'd wanted it for so long."

I hugged Mom and nuzzled up to her. "It will be good, Mom. Don't worry."

"Thanks, Bern. You're my sweetheart."

"Want some raisins?"

"Sure, give me a handful."

"Is Gabe coming back?"

Mom looked at me. "I would imagine so," she said dryly. "He has to eat too."

A Visit from Grandma

Jonah's coming back in two weeks. Hurray! I wrote him sixteen letters, or rather I typed them because it's easier. You'd think it wouldn't be good writing letters to someone and not getting answers, but I don't mind because I know Jonah so well I can imagine what he would write back if he did. Anyhow, it's not *his* fault he's not good at writing. He's good at some other things, but not at writing.

It's amazing how well Suzu can talk now. She's been living in our house three months—it's August now—and she can talk really well. Mom says the younger a child is, the faster she will catch on. I ask Suzu sometimes about her life in Vietnam, but she doesn't seem to remember that much. Once she said she had a brother, another time she said she had three brothers! She likes to call me Berry, even though she knows my real name now. When she was eating blackberries, she said, "Berry, I eat you!" and laughed.

I decided to try and teach her the alphabet for school, but Mom says she's too young. At the end of the month she'll be five. When I tell her that, she says, "No, I be 'leven." She knows I'm eleven. I guess she wants to be me. In fact, I think she thinks she'll be in my class at school.

"You can't be eleven. You'll be five," I said.

"Eventually you'll be eleven," Mom said. "One day. But first you'll have to be five."

"No, I 'leven," Suzu said. She's pretty stubborn at times.

Mom said Grandma is coming for Suzu's birthday. She and Gabe are going away for a weekend and Grandma will stay with us. I love it when Grandma comes to stay. Before Mom married Gabe, whenever she had to go away for her job, Grandma would stay with me. She's never even seen Suzu, except in those pictures the adoption agency sent us a long time ago. Suzu is much cuter now. Mom got her these plastic barrettes in different colors and every day she puts one on to match what Suzu is wearing. Lots of times when we go shopping, people smile at her and say something about how cute she is. She looks a lot like me. In fact, she looks more like me than Zachary looks like Jonah, so people never think she's adopted. They think she's my real sister.

Only she's cuter than I used to be when I was little. I don't care. It's O.K. not to be cute.

"Grandma's coming," I said to Suzu. Of course, she doesn't know who Grandma is. I showed her these pictures of grandma dolls in an FAO Schwarz catalogue we have, but I think she just thought our real Grandma was a doll and that it was a present she was getting. Mom said she and Gabe are getting Suzu a Jumbo elephant and a Weebles marina. She saw that Weebles marina on TV and said she wanted it. The thing is, she always says she wants what she sees on TV, even if it's not something you can buy. Even if she sees, like, a person, she'll say to me, "Buy for me, Berry?" So I say "Yes," because it's too complicated to explain. She must think I'm a millionaire or something.

I miss Grandma. She lives in Chicago, only she doesn't live with Grandpa anymore because he married someone else. I wish Mom went on trips more with her job and Grandma could stay with us, even if Gabe was here. But Gabe doesn't like Grandma. Apart from calling her Moaner and Groaner, he says she gets on his nerves. Mom said once that men never like the mothers of the women they marry and it's too complicated to explain. But then I asked her didn't Dad like Grandma, because he never calls her names, and she said Yes, that was true, there were exceptions to every rule.

Anyway, I'm really excited about seeing

Grandma again. She's so pretty! She's really a cute little grandma. She dyes her hair such a pretty color—it's sort of reddish blond—and I love her dresses. She has pierced ears and lots of beautiful earrings.

"This is Suzu, Mother," Mom said when we met Grandma at the airport. Mom had gotten Suzu all cleaned and dressed up in this red-and-white dress. She wouldn't wear her shoes because she always says they're too slippery, so she had her sneakers on, but otherwise she looked really nice. I just had on shorts and a sleeveless blouse because Grandma knows all about me.

"She's big!" Suzu said to me. She looked almost scared, like she had imagined Grandma would be tiny, like that dollhouse grandma doll.

"She's Mommy's mother," I said.

Suzu looked at Mom. I guess she couldn't imagine Mom had a mother.

"Hi, Suzu," Grandma said. "My, you're a big girl."

"I be 'leven," Suzu said.

"She likes to say that," I said to Grandma. "Really, she's going to be five."

"Well, five is a splendid age," Grandma said. "I wouldn't mind being five myself."

I would. I wouldn't like to be five again. I guess Grandma says that because really she doesn't remember. There's so much stuff you're not allowed to do when you're five.

"You be five?" Suzu said to Grandma.

I laughed. "No, dum-dum, she's around sixty-five."

"Sixty-two," Grandma said. "Don't rush me, Bernie."

"You look marvelous," Mom said, taking Grandma's bag.

"Well, I feel pretty good. You're a little thin, aren't you, Becka? You look tired."

"Oh, well, no, I'm O.K.," Mom said.

"How's Gabe?"

"Oh . . . pretty good. You know, he wasn't rehired for next year."

"He wasn't?"

"Uh uh. The college says they just can't afford putting any more people on tenure. It's so rotten, really, because he's worked so damn hard."

"What a shame," said Grandma. "What will he *do?*"

"Well, look for something else, I guess," Mom said. "But—you know, like if he seems in a funny mood, it's because of that."

"Oh, of *course,*" Grandma said. "I understand perfectly. Why, that's just terrible. Isn't there anything you can do?"

"He just found out over the summer," Mom said. We all got into the car. "He was fired is what it boils down to, though they like to dodge the issue with a lot of fancy words."

"Fire?" Suzu said. "Daddy on fire?"

34

"No, it's something completely different," I said. "You're too little to understand."

"I'm really so sorry to hear this," Grandma said. "What terrible news."

"Well, don't make too big a deal of it. You know how sensitive he is."

"I know, I *know*."

"Anyway, it could be a blessing in disguise. Gabe would really like to take a year off and sculpt."

"Mom, will we have to leave New York and move somewhere else?"

"No, hon, don't be silly. Please, don't worry about it."

"I don't want to move. I love New York. And Jonah's here—and everything!"

"Cool it, Bern. We're not moving. We're staying right here where we are."

"You know, *I'm* a working woman now," Grandma said. "What do you think of that?"

"Hey, that's right," Mom said. "Are you still with that health food store? Do you still like it?"

"I am and I love it!" Grandma said. "Would you believe it? I never worked a day in my life and I *love* it. I'm in charge of herbs."

"In charge in what sense?"

"Well, these young people come in—it's a store mostly frequented by young people—and they want to know which herbs to use and I tell them."

"How much do you get?" Mom asked.

"Well, I don't really know," Grandma said and laughed.

"What?" Mom was driving so she couldn't turn around and stare at Grandma, but you could tell she wanted to. "You don't know what you're paid?"

"Now, Becka, I'm sure they're fair. They're not out to cheat me, after all. But it's a new place, they just opened, and they've had problems with the mortgage and it's not like I'm destitute. I do get paid, but it's in relation to what the store takes in."

"That's disgraceful!" Mom said. "They're probably cheating you *blind!"*

"No, of course they're not!" Grandma took my hand. "Why does your mother get so excited over trifles?" she said.

"Look, it's great you're working," Mom said, "but don't let them *do* that to you. Get whatever you're worth."

"I don't know that I'm worth that much."

"Garbage!"

"Garbage?" Suzu said.

"Mom, calm down," I said.

"What am I worth, Bernie?" Grandma said, squeezing me.

"You're worth infinity dollars and infinity cents."

Back at the house Grandma, Mom, and Suzu went into the kitchen to have lemonade. I didn't feel that thirsty. "Can I type, Mom?"

"Sure, hon. It's going to be hot up there, though."

"I'll take my shirt off."

I decided to write about two little girls who run away from home. I once ran away when I was six, but only for three hours. Then I got hungry.

When I came down for supper, I brought my notebook because I wanted to show it to Grandma—not just what I did today, but all my stuff.

"Grandma, here," I said when we were done eating.

"What's that?"

"It's my notebook. It's all my stories that I typed."

Grandma opened it slowly. "You typed all this yourself?"

"Uh huh."

"For school?"

"No, just for fun."

"But this is several hundred pages!"

"Oh, this is just the one for 1974. I have some others for 1973 and 1972 and—"

"Hon, go take your bath with Suzu . . . Grandma can look at your notebook while you're in the bath."

"Do I *have* to?"

"Of course you do."

"But Suzu had a bath already."

"You know she likes to have one with you."

Suzu really loves taking a bath with me. I like it too most of the time, except she splashes on the floor and she's not supposed to. I make her ice-cream drinks out of soapsuds and she really eats them. We put all these rubber dolls in a boat and pretend they're going on a trip. Usually I get out first and she likes to stay in a real long time, even if she had a bath before. She really loves being in the bath!

"Did you read it yet?" I ran into the living room.

"Bern, put on your nightgown," Mom yelled.

I ran back. As I was putting it on, I heard Grandma say, "But does she get lots of fresh air and eat well?"

"Of course!" Mom said.

"And she has friends her own age?"

"Do you mean me?" I said, coming back with my nightgown on my head.

"Bern, I said get *into* it. Now I mean it!"

"I'm just a little worried," Grandma said, "at all of this." She patted my notebook.

"Which is your favorite part?" I said, snuggling up to her.

"How did you learn all this? All this spelling and punctuation?"

"I don't know, I just did."

Grandma wasn't even reading it! She just sat there, kind of leafing through it. "I don't know," she kept saying in this worried voice. "You're only eleven years old."

"That doesn't matter, Grandma," I said. I felt

really awful. She acted like I'd done some really bad thing.

Grandma took my hand and said, "You should be out playing, sweetheart. Not cooped up like this—"

I jerked away and went outside. I felt like I was going to cry. You'd think she'd at least read what I'd written. What does she care if I want to type? I'm not hurting anyone, am I?

A long while later Mom came out in the yard. She wandered over to where I was sitting and said, "Grandma does like your notebook, hon."

"She does *not!* She didn't even *read* it!"

"Well, she is now."

"Well, what's so bad about it?" I said. That feeling like I was going to cry came back. "She acted like I did some really bad thing."

Mom sighed. "It's hard to explain, Bern. Grown-ups, well, I guess they look back on when they were children and wish they'd taken advantage of it more. Because when you're grown up, you can't fool around and play quite so much. You have to work and look after your children. So Grandma's just afraid that you're not doing all that and that later, when you're grown up, you'll regret it."

"But I *like* to type."

"I know you do. Hon, it's great you do. It is, really. Grandma's awfully proud of you. It's just that she wants you to be happy."

I nodded. "O.K.," I said. "Can I go type now?"

Mom laughed. "Well, why don't we hold off for tonight? It's almost eight and I want to get Suzu into bed."

"Is she still in her bath?"

"Yup."

"She'll get all wrinkly," I said. I hate it when that happens and your skin is puckered.

Honey, Ya Can't Love One

"How do I look?" Jonah said. He just got back yesterday, but he came over to say hello.

"Good. You got tan." I didn't think he looked that much thinner, but I couldn't tell.

He lowered his voice. "I gained seven pounds."

"Well, seven isn't so bad."

"Mom's going to faint when she finds out. When I got off the train, she must've thought I looked thinner because she kept saying how great I looked and how I must've had a wonderful time. I didn't really say anything because I figured why wreck it for her."

"*Didn't* you have a wonderful time?"

"It wasn't bad. Thanks for writing me all those letters." He looked embarrassed. "The thing is, I hope you don't mind, Bern. I told all the guys you were a boy. Bernie sounds more like a boy's name, anyhow."

"Sure, that's O.K.," I said.

"If they knew you were a girl, they might've, you know, teased me. There was this one boy who got letters from a girl with perfume on them and stuff and they kept calling him lover boy."

"That's really stupid," I said. "Just because one person is a boy and one person is a girl, doesn't mean it's some big romance."

"I know. But they figure it means you're always kissing and doing things like that."

I made a face. "I wouldn't put perfume on a letter if I lived to be one million years old," I said. "You can depend on that."

It seemed like summer vacation went by fast this year. The only really special thing was Grandma's coming to visit. It's funny, but even though Suzu has only been living with us less than half a year, I can't remember that well what it was like before we had her. She started school and everything and she even has dates afterward. She got pretty mad when she saw we wouldn't be in the same class and she started to scream like she used to do in the beginning. But when she got used to it, she was O.K. The only thing is, I think she thinks I'm just going to stay in the same class I'm in now till *she's* eleven and then we'll be in the same class all the time. Well, I suppose by then she'll have figured it out.

I don't think it helped that much for Mom and

Gabe to go away that time by themselves. There's still a lot of fighting. In fact, it's worse. Last night they were in the kitchen and Mom started saying something about how Gabe shouldn't worry about not being able to find a job because now he could just do his sculpture like he always wanted.

"And live off you?" Gabe said. "The hell with that!"

Mom said it wasn't a matter of anyone living *off* anyone. She said if she didn't have a job and had some special project she wanted to work on, she wouldn't mind letting him support her.

Gabe said that was completely different.

Mom said how was it different?

Gabe said it was obvious how. For a man to live off a woman was just completely different from a woman to live off a man.

"It's not!" Mom said. "It's exactly the same!"

"Bullshit!" Gabe said. "It's a whole thing of pride and an attitude toward work and don't give me that it's just the same business."

"Women have just as much pride as men," Mom said.

"O.K., everything is the same," Gabe said. "Men are exactly like women. No differences at all. Fine."

"Look, if you want to spend the year killing yourself trying to get a job, do it!" Mom said. "That's your option."

Gabe said she just wanted to close her eyes to the fact that creating a piece of sculpture was not

43

the same as waltzing in and picking up a paycheck once a month.

Mom said she did *not* waltz in and pick up a paycheck. She said she put her whole goddamn heart and soul into her work and if he regarded that as "waltzing in," he didn't understand the first thing about it.

Anyway, it went on for quite a long time like that. The funny thing about people when they argue is they never stick to one point. They say one thing and then they go off on something else and that just keeps happening until I guess they just get too tired to do it anymore. Sometimes I feel like yelling out, "But you never answered that" or "You said the opposite a few minutes ago," but I know they'd just get mad at me for butting in or for listening in the first place, so finally I just put the blanket over my head and try to think up some story I can type the next day.

The really surprising thing is Suzu sleeps through it all. She really sleeps like a log. Only the next night after they had the argument about whether there were any differences between men and women, they had a fight in front of Suzu.

It was after supper. Gabe and Mom were eating in the dining room by themselves, like they usually do, and Suzu was still in the bath. I came in to get a snack and then Suzu came in. She didn't have any clothes on and she was all wet.

"Get into your jamers," Mom said.

"No!" Suzu yelled. "Want to be naked."

"Look, I don't care if she's naked or dressed in a snowsuit," Gabe said. "I just want to eat dinner in peace."

Then Suzu noticed they were having watermelon. "*I* want some," she said.

"O.K., you can have a little of mine," Mom said.

"Want to sit on lap," Suzu said and she climbed up. "Ooh, take out seeds!"

So Mom began taking the seeds out for Suzu and playing a game where she would say, "Come on out, you seed. What're you doing hiding there? You get out." Suzu kept giggling and munching away and Gabe kept staring at them like they were crazy.

"Look!" Suzu said.

"What are you doing?" Mom said.

I looked and Mom looked and Gabe looked. She was putting her foot in her vagina.

"Now what is that foot doing there?" Mom said. "That vagina says, 'Get out, foot! You leave me alone.'"

"No hair on tookie," Suzu said.

"On what?" said Mom.

"Tookie," Suzu said. "That's my tookie."

I felt sort of embarrassed. "That's this word for vagina . . . They use it at school."

"Well, that's ridiculous. Don't teach her that kind of idiocy, Bernie! Teach her the regular names."

"It's not *my* fault! I didn't teach it to her."

"Well, if you hear her picking up stuff like that, correct her," Mom snorted. "Tookie!"

Gabe said, "Do you think it would be possible to interrupt this fascinating conversation and have a cup of coffee?"

Mom started to get up, but Suzu said, "Want coffee."

"Suzu, honey, coffee is a drink for grown-ups," Mom said. "You wouldn't like it. It's bitter."

"Want coffee," Suzu said.

"Becka, I am going to count to three and if that child is not out of this room, I am going to wallop her to kingdom come. I am just sick of this! Now scram!"

Suzu just stared at Gabe.

Mom said, "You are not laying one finger on her!"

"The hell I'm not!"

But just as Gabe got out of his chair, Mom grabbed Suzu and took her off to the other room. I just stood there, eating my watermelon and minding my own business.

"Hey, quit looking at me with those knowing black eyes," Gabe said. "You're turning into a little old lady."

"Well, *you're* turning into a mean, ugly stepfather," I said. I put the watermelon down on the table and walked out. I didn't feel that much like finishing it, to tell the truth.

Suzu was in our room crying. Mom was hugging her, saying, "Pooch, Daddy is tired, that's all."

"He'll hit me," Suzu wailed.

"No, he won't," Mom said. "I can promise you that. Now, tuck in, girls. It's getting late."

"I'm never getting married," I said.

"O.K., let's not get into that now," Mom said. "Let's just be two good girls and go to sleep. There's school tomorrow, remember?"

"You *sing,*" Suzu said after Mom went out.

Suzu's favorite song is one I learned at camp last summer. It goes, "Honey, ya can't love one! Oh you can't love one and still have fun, I'm leaving on the midnight line, Yah Dah Dah, Hoo Hoo!" I sang it a little, but I was sort of tired.

The next day I asked Jonah if his parents ever have fights. He said they do only his father never fights back so it's not a real fight. He said his father said he's a pacifist and doesn't believe in fighting. "Does your mother believe in it?" I said.

"I don't know if she believes in it, but she does it," he said.

Going to Boston

At the beginning of November something exciting happened. I got this letter from Dad saying he was going to Boston to get married and he and his girlfriend, Peggy, wondered if I could come and stay with them for the wedding. He said they especially wanted me to be at their wedding, even though it would be small.

"Can I go, Mom? Please, pretty pretty please?"

"Well, sure, I guess. But, are you up to traveling by yourself? I could put you on the train and have him pick you up." She looked worried.

"I can. I don't mind."

"*I* want to go," Suzu said.

"Well, you can't, it's *my* father. You don't even know him."

Suzu started to cry. Mom looked at me with

this angry expression. "Bernie, use your head! She doesn't understand that."

"I want two Daddies too," Suzu said.

"Boy, does Suzu have to go *everywhere* I do? It's not fair."

"You'll go alone," Mom said that night, "but be nice to Suzu, Bern. Please."

"I *am* nice to her."

"You're sort of like another mother to her. She'll miss you a lot if you go away for a weekend. Which I don't say means you shouldn't go, but just realize that."

"I could bring her back a present."

"That would be nice."

The odd thing was Gabe got mad about my going. I never expected that. It seemed he had this show of his sculpture in the college museum which was opening that weekend.

"Doesn't she want to go?" he asked Mom.

"Of course she does," Mom said. "But it'll run after she's back."

"But I thought we'd all go to the opening together."

Mom sighed. "Look, it's her father and she doesn't see him much and—"

"Sure, I'm just this guy who happens to hang around here," Gabe said.

"Gabe, obviously this is different. Don't pretend you can't see that."

"O.K., forget it. Suzu will go," Gabe said. "How about it, Suzu? You want to come?" Ever since that night when Gabe said he would hit Suzu, he's been acting extra nice to make up to her, but she still seems scared of him.

There's just one reason I don't feel that much like going to Boston right now. That's because I'm working on this really long story called "Mamie and the Hebrew War." It's going to have chapters and everything. It's for older children. Only now I'll have to stop in the middle.

"Do you think Dad and Peggy will have a typewriter?" I asked Mom.

"Sweetheart, you can stop typing for one weekend. Now, let's not let this turn into an obsession."

"What's that?"

"It's something where you can't stop doing it."

"Oh, O.K."

But the week before I left, I went up to the study after supper to write part of it just so I could get started. I'm taking a few stories to show Dad and Peggy, not this one because it's not even finished, just some short other ones I once did.

"You're really lucky," Jonah said when I told him about my trip. "Your parents are great."

"What's so lucky?" I said.

"Going to Boston all by yourself. Mine would never let me."

"Oh, come on, sure they would. You're eleven."

"I know! Only when I told them about you going, I heard my mother say to my father how she thought it was so irresponsible of your mother to let you go by yourself."

"You mean because of robbers and muggers and stuff?"

"I guess."

"Well, my mother says your mother is over-protective and that it's bad for you." Jonah looked glum like he agreed so I said, "Maybe you could come? Do you think your mother would let you?"

"Come to Boston?"

"Yeah. Hey, it would be great. And we wouldn't be alone, we'd be together."

"She'd never let me."

"Ask her. We can say we'll go to museums and stuff so it'll be educational."

"But how about your father? I thought you said he was getting married."

"So? You can come. It's not the kind where people get all dressed up. I think you just go down to this place where there's a judge. It's not all fancy."

But both our mothers said No. Jonah's mother didn't seem to think going together, just the two of us, was that much better than going alone, and Mom said she thought Dad wanted it to be more intimate and since he didn't even know Jonah, that might spoil it. Anyway, at least I'm still going. That's *something*.

Suzu and Mom took me to Grand Central. I waved at them out the window. Suzu was crying, but Mom kept hugging her. I guess Suzu will

51

miss me, but I'll be back Sunday. I tried to tell her about that, but I don't think she knows about time that well. I think I'll send Jonah a postcard. I really feel excited! I wonder what Peggy will be like. I asked Mom, but she said how should she know, she never saw her. I asked if Dad had written her he was going to get married, but Mom said No, didn't I know he wasn't like that.

The thing is, Dad writes really good letters, but he never says things like exactly what he's doing. He more describes some scene or draws a little picture, stuff like that. I imagine Peggy will be sort of strong looking with glasses and maybe red hair.

This lady I was sitting next to on the train saw me waving at Suzu and Mom so I told her that was my baby sister from Vietnam. I told her how we adopted her and all that.

"She's crying because I'm going away and she'll miss me a lot. But she's too little to come, she'd just wreck it. Anyway, Dad isn't even her real father so there's no reason she should go."

"Is he *your* real father?" the lady said. She was in a white suit and her blouse had black apples on it.

"Well, he used to be," I said. "He still is, really . . . but he's going to marry Peggy. Mom doesn't mind because she's married to Gabe."

"I see," the lady said. After a minute she added, "Gabe must be your stepfather, then?"

"Yeah, he's not that nice lately, though."

The lady looked worried. "In what way?"

"Well, he uses bad language. And he yells and screams a lot."

"I'm sorry," the lady said. "I'm really sorry to hear that."

"Mom says it's because he lost his job, and he's a sculptor so he has an artistic temperament, but so what? He should still act nice. I'm a writer, but I'm still nice."

"Oh, what do you write?" asked the lady.

I told her about my stories. "I brought some, but they're in my suitcase . . . I'm going to be a writer when I grow up."

"Well, isn't that a coincidence," the lady said. "*I'm* a writer."

"You are?" I was really excited. I never met a real writer before. "Are you famous?"

"No, not really. Well, mostly I'm a ghost writer."

"*I* write scary stories sometimes . . . Jonah likes those best."

"Oh, well, you see, a ghost writer is something different. You don't write about ghosts. It means if someone wants to write a book and they don't know how, they ask you to write it for them."

"What was the name of your last book?" I asked her.

She smiled. "*Diseases of the Scalp*. It was for a doctor."

"Oh." That didn't sound that interesting, but I didn't want to hurt the lady's feelings. "My latest book is called "Mamie and the Hebrew War." It's not finished yet. It's going to be really long and have chapters and everything."

"Are you Jewish?" asked the lady.

"Half . . . from my mother. Only we're not religious like Cynthia. That's our babysitter. She's going to be a rabbi."

"Your mother must be really proud of you, knowing what you want to do already."

"I don't know," I said. "I guess she is."

"I'm sure she is."

"The thing is, I wish I could sell my book and make money. To make up for Gabe losing his job."

"Does your mother work?"

"Yes, she's on TV. Sometimes she's on the six o'clock news, if you ever watch that."

The lady's eyes opened wide. "She isn't that young woman, the one with the curly hair who does those human interest stories?"

"Yeah, that's her."

"Goodness! Yes, I remember. She did that story some time back on hard-to-place children. Well, you tell your mommy I'm a big fan of hers."

I nodded. "See, what I keep worrying about is they might come and take Suzu back to Vietnam. Because they might think she's in an unsettled home, if they heard all the fighting that goes on and stuff."

"Oh, I'm sure that won't happen."

"It might. Only, I guess I could try and hide

Suzu. The trouble is, then they might put *me* in jail."

The lady patted my arm. "You're much too young to be doing so much worrying, dear," she said with a laugh.

I don't know why grown-ups say things like that. You can worry just as much if you're eleven as if you're a hundred. They probably worried about millions of things when they were eleven, but now they just don't remember. Well, I'm going to remember, even if I live longer than a hundred. I'm never going to forget one single thing.

Dad and Peggy Get Married

"You're so big!" Peggy said.

She was really different from what I expected. She had curly blond hair and pink skin. Her dress was red and pink and purple stripes. I think she must have a baby in her or else she's pretty fat. She looked like her name should be Piggy.

"What kind of food do you feel like?" Dad said.

"Italian," I said. I like all kinds of noodles.

So we went back to the hotel to wash up and then we ate out. In the hotel room Dad and Peggy had put their mattress right on the floor because Peggy said they liked to sleep that way. When we came back, she said I could have my mattress on the floor too, but I said I was more used to it the other way.

"You look like you might be going to have a baby," I said.

"Yes, lord, it's due in two months. Aren't I *huge?*"

"What do you hope it is?" I said.

"Anything . . . I just want it to be born." She was taking off her dress. I guess I never saw a pregnant lady naked before. They really look funny. "*He* thinks I'm gorgeous," she said, pointing to Dad as she went in to shower. "*I* think I look like a hippo."

I wonder why Dad never wrote that he and Peggy were going to have a baby. "When are you getting married?" I asked him.

"Tomorrow's the big day."

"Am I really going to be a bridesmaid?" I always wanted to be, but no one ever asked me.

"Well, it's just a little wedding, Bernie. But we wanted you to be there."

I showed him a photo of Suzu that Gabe took. She was in her Oshkosh overalls and navy blue turtleneck.

"Well, she certainly looks thoroughly Americanized," Dad said.

"Do you like her?" I asked.

"I think I would. You all ought to come out and see us some day."

"I don't think we have enough money," I said. I didn't know if I should tell Dad about Gabe losing his job.

Peggy came out of the bathroom wrapped in

a big towel. She looked at the photo. "She's darling," she said. "If we have a girl, I hope she looks just like that . . . those big black eyes. She looks just like you, Bernie."

"I know, it's funny since she's adopted."

"Well, they say people get to look like each other." She sneezed.

"God bless you," I said.

"I *pray* I'm not getting a cold. Maybe I'm allergic to getting married."

"How come you didn't get married before this?"

"She wouldn't," Dad said. "*I* wanted to. She said she didn't believe in it."

"No," Peggy said, laughing. "I do . . . I was too busy, was all. I'm a filmmaker, and I was right in the middle of a project."

"I don't believe in marriage either," I said. "I'm *never* getting married."

"These liberated women," Dad said. "What are we men going to do with you?"

"Why don't you want to get married?" Peggy said. She was the kind of person who really seemed to listen to everything you said. Dad is like that too. He's very quiet, but he always remembers everything you tell him. Not like Mom —she forgets lots of things.

"When people get married, they always fight," I said.

Peggy didn't say anything. She just stood looking at me in this funny way.

"You were never married before so maybe you don't know," I said.

She still didn't say anything so I said, "What will you name your baby?"

"I think Hoshi after Fumio's mother if it's a girl and Jacob after my father if it's a boy."

I told them about my *New Age Baby Name Book* and how I picked the name Suzu. "I'm writing my own baby name book too," I said. "It's called the *Super Hero Name Your Baby Book*."

"Fumio tells me you're quite a writer," Peggy said.

"I brought you some stories if you want to see them."

"I'd love to."

I showed them the one about Erica, the girl with the purple hair. I did pictures for that, but I didn't bring them.

Peggy sat down cross-legged in her bathrobe and read my story. "Did you *really* write that, Bernie?"

"Sure, do you like it?"

"Your mother must have helped you."

That made me mad. "Mom never even *saw* this!"

"I like the part about the Daddy giving her maple walnut ice milk," Dad said. He was reading it now. "That's nice."

"You're a genius! My God!" Peggy said. "I'm

59

scared of you." To Dad she said, "Why didn't you tell me she was a genius?"

The wedding was in this place called City Hall. It was just us and Peggy's mother. Peggy started to giggle at one point, but then she stopped. She said she was nervous. When it was over, she kissed me and hugged me and started to cry. "Help! I'm legal!" she said.

"Well, don't have the baby right here," her mother said. To me she said, "Now you have a stepmother."

"You better not be wicked like the ones in the fairy tales."

"Yeah, you're right. I better start practicing up on wicked stuff," Peggy said.

We went to this place where they had champagne. I had a little, but then they said I could have a Coke so I did. Suddenly Dad said, "Everyone's going to think I'm crazy, but you know what I feel like doing right now?"

We all looked at him.

"Ice skating!" he said.

"Why not?" Peggy said.

He looked at her and at her big stomach. "Are you up to it, honey?"

"Are you kidding? I can't ice skate anyhow. No, I'll watch. I like to watch you skate."

I like to watch Dad ice skate too. It's his favorite sport. When he was little, he used to do it all the time. He's good at other sports too, like

swimming and tennis, but he says ice skating is
his favorite. I rented some skates too, but I'm
not good like Dad. My ankles sort of cave in and
I have to keep going over to the rail to hang on.
I stopped there, watching Dad skimming around
in the middle where the good skaters go. He was
wearing black slacks and a black turtleneck
sweater and he looked sort of like a dancer, just
gliding back and forth. I noticed some people
were watching him, probably wishing they could
do as well. There was a little girl who looked
around six in a short red skirt. She was good too,
but more in a show-offy way, like she knew people were watching her. She would do fancy stuff
like bending down and twirling around and then
would kind of smile. But Dad didn't even seem
to know people were watching him. He skated
over to me. "Let's skate together," he said.

"I'm rotten," I said.

"No, you're just too self-conscious, Bern. Don't
look down at your feet. They know what to do.
Your feet know a lot more than you do."

"They do?"

When you skate with someone who's really
good, like Dad, you feel like you're good too.
You feel light, almost as if you were flying. We
skated past Peggy and she waved.

"Hi, Peggy!" I yelled. I tried to wave, but that
made me almost lose my balance.

"It would be great if you could come out and

stay with us," Dad said. "Would Becka let you?
I think you could fly alone by now."

"Sure!" I said. I didn't really mean to say this,
but suddenly I said, "I miss you a lot, Daddy."

"I miss you too, sweetheart—all the time. I'm
sorry my letters aren't that good."

"Jonah's letters aren't good either," I said. "I
guess men don't like to write letters."

"Why don't you call me sometimes?"

"Wouldn't that be horribly expensive?"

"No. I should have thought of that before. Do
you know how to call collect?"

"Uh uh."

"Well, when we get back to the hotel, I'll
explain it to you. Then, whenever you feel like
talking to me, you just pick up the phone. I'll
give you my work number too."

My toes were getting cold, but it was so nice
skating with Dad that I didn't want to stop. "Gabe
doesn't like sports," I said. "He thinks they're
dumb."

"Becka is happy, though?" Dad said. "I mean,
she and Gabe—"

I looked at him. I felt scared, like I knew I
shouldn't say anything, but I couldn't help it.
"No, it's awful, they aren't happy," I said. "They
fight all the time. Ever since Suzu came." I tried
not to cry, but tears started coming down. They
felt cold from the cold air. "They yell and they—"

"Poor darling," Dad said. I could feel my
ankles sort of collapsing, but he held me up.

"You poor thing. You shouldn't have to be aware of all that."

"It's him," I said. "It's not Mom. He used to be nice, but now I hate him. Suzu hates him too. He said he'd wallop her to kingdom come."

"Jesus," Dad said. He looked angry. "You should have written me, Bernie. Why didn't you? I had no idea."

"Dad, please don't tell Mom I told you. Do you swear?"

"You think she'd—"

"Please, promise?"

"Of course I won't tell her, if you don't want me to. But let's arrange a good long visit for you soon. Maybe we could think of having you live with us for a while until things . . . get resolved."

"You mean till they get divorced?"

"Well, whatever. Remember, Bernie, we have lots of room. We would love to have you."

I nodded. I couldn't quite imagine moving to a completely different place without Jonah or Suzu or Mom. "I'll think about it," I said, sniffing. I felt better.

We skated back to where Peggy was. "Hey, you were terrific," Peggy said. "It must be in the genes. The minute I touch ice, I fall on my butt."

"I'm not really that good," I said, knowing she wouldn't believe me. But Dad just smiled and squeezed my hand. I wish Dad didn't have to live so far away. Lots of people have parents who are divorced but the father picks them up every weekend like Marjorie Mangold's father does. It's not fair! If I could see Dad every weekend, I wouldn't mind about Gabe and Mom.

The next day they took me to the train station. Dad was sort of quiet. He'd explained to me about calling collect and wrote it down on a piece of paper. Peggy said to me, "So Bernie, it's settled? You're coming to stay with us? We want you to! We'll send you a letter."

"O.K.," I said.

"We'll have a ball," she said. "I could show you how to make movies. How'd you like that?"

"I would."

"It'll be terrific." She laughed and wiped her forehead. "I have a feeling Bernie knows a lot more about babies than I do. I'm going to need you, kid."

"We *would* like to have you," Dad said in this real quiet voice.

"O.K.!" I said. "Would I have to fly?"

"It would be easier. Would you be scared?"

"I don't know. I never did it."

On the train on the way home I kept thinking about how nice Peggy was. She does look a little like a pig, but in a nice way, like one of those clean pink pigs with round little noses that you see in the movies. I didn't know if I should tell Mom how much I liked Peggy because she might be jealous. That lady that was on the train with

64

me going to Boston wasn't there going back. I sat next to this boy who didn't talk very much. But I didn't mind because I had a lot of things to think about.

The Bridesmaid
Returns Home

"So, bridesmaid of the month, how did it go?"
Mom said. We were going home in a cab. Suzu
was sitting in the middle. "We missed you, didn't
we, Suzu?"

Suzu just nodded and pressed up next to me.

"She was really nice," I said. "She said I should
come out and live with them. She's going to send
me a ticket. I'll fly, I guess."

"What? What are you talking about?"

"Peggy. She said she really needs me because
she doesn't know much about babies."

"So? Why does she have to know about
babies?"

"Well, she's having one in two months so of
course she has to know!" I said.

"What?"

66

"But, Mom, they didn't have time to get married before because she was making these movies."

"Wait a sec. You mean she's pregnant? Seven months pregnant?"

"Uh huh."

"This is weird . . . I can't believe it."

"It was good, Mom, really. She's very nice. You'd like her."

"I bet I would."

"She said I was a genius. I showed her some of my stories."

"Excuse me if I'm going to be sick," Mom said.

"What's wrong?"

"She certainly buttered you up enough!"

"It wasn't like that. She was a very sincere person." Sometimes Mom really gets me mad.

"Well, go live with them, then!" Mom said. "Great! Suzu and I will manage just fine."

"Mom, come on! We just talked about it. It's not definite. It's just for a visit."

"Look, do whatever you like. It's up to you."

I didn't say anything because you could tell Mom was in some kind of crazy mood. "Where's Gabe?" I asked when we got home.

"He went on a trip," Mom said.

"Where to?"

Suddenly Mom whirled around. "He just went on a fucking trip!" she yelled. "Bern, will you quit bugging me! Do you have to know every single thing in the whole wide world?"

"You said a dirty word, Mom."

"I mean it, Bern! Leave me alone!"

"O.K., can I go type?"

"No, you can't! You're back in this house exactly one minute and you're typing already! Play with Suzu!"

"Will you pay me ten cents a book if I read to her?"

"No!"

"Then I won't do it."

"Wow, what a sweet kid I gave birth to. How did I manage it?"

"You play with me," Suzu said, yanking on my arm. "I need you to play with me."

So I played with Suzu. Boy, talking about lousy moods! I've seen Mom mad lots of times, but this was one of the worst. Anyway, I never said I was going to live with Dad and Peggy *all* the time.

Suzu and I played this game with her stuffed animals, Gray Mouse and Fluffy the Cat. "You bug me," Suzu said to the cat. "Bug! Bug!"

I did read her some books. You can't exactly read to Suzu in the regular way. I mean, she won't let you read the real words because she holds the book and turns the pages quite fast. We read *Horton Hears a Who*. She really likes the part where they're going to put the speck in beezlenut oil. Then she wanted to watch TV so I turned on Sesame. I went in to go to the bathroom and when I came back, she was asleep.

"Hey, Mom, Suzu's asleep. Can I type now?"

"O.K."

I went up to write about Mamie and the Hebrew War. I typed for about half an hour and then I decided to go down and see what Mom was cooking for supper. When I went downstairs, the light was off in the kitchen. I looked in the living room and Suzu was still sleeping on the floor. It made me kind of scared to have all the lights out.

"Mom?"

"I'm in here, hon. I'm lying down."

I went where her voice was, in her bedroom. Mom had the quilt over her. I love that quilt. When I was little, we used to play this game with it where we'd spread it on the floor and we'd throw our slippers around. I used to call my slippers Gorgeous Gussies, I forget why.

"I felt a little tired," Mom said in this low voice.

"Can I tuck in with you?"

"Sure."

We lay there in the dark. It was really black and cold looking out the window, a little bit scary.

"Mom, did you know there was something called a ghost writer? I met this lady on the train who was one. You have to write about things like diseases of the scalp."

"Umm," Mom said, as though she wasn't really listening.

I hugged her. "You're the nicest mommy in the whole wide world."

"Oh, Bern! Don't say that! I'm not! I'm bad!"

"No, you're not. What's so bad about you?"

"I don't even know where Gabe *is*. He just went."

"Do you miss him?"

"Oh, hon, I don't know, I just don't. If you go live with Dad and Peggy, I don't know what I'll do!"

"It would just be for a visit. It wouldn't be for always."

"No, but you'd go there and you'd like it and you'd have this exciting great life and you'd live in a dome and she'd be making movies and you'd never want to come back."

"Mom, don't be silly."

"How would I manage Suzu? She adores you. You're practically like her mother."

"We could all go," I said.

"Where? To California? But my job is here, hon, and all my friends. It's not so easy."

"Mom, I know you don't like Peggy, but you would if you met her. I bet anything you would."

"I don't *not* like her!"

"No, but you'd really *like* her. Do you mind that she was pregnant when she got married?"

"Why should I?"

"But, would you do that?"

70

"No, I guess I'm just too conventional, Bern. But I admire people like that, I really do."

"If it's a girl, they're going to call her Hoshi."

"That's pretty." Mom yawned.

"Will we be poor now that Gabe has left?"

"He *hasn't* left!"

"You said you didn't know where he was."

"We're not poor," Mom said slowly. "I mean, we're not *rich,* but with my job——"

"I wish I could publish my books and make lots of money."

"You don't need to."

"I *want* to! Maybe I'll send them out to some publisher."

"Honey, don't go on some fantasy trip about money. We'll make it."

Suddenly my stomach growled. "I'm hungry," I said.

"O.K., let's eat."

"Should I wake up Suzu?"

"Maybe she'll sleep straight through," Mom said. She yawned again and shook her head.

"She'll be grumpy if we wake her up."

"Let's not then. Listen, tell me about the wedding, Bern. You never did. What was it like?"

I told her.

71

Grandma Meets
a Lovely Widower

Gabe didn't come back.

Mom seemed sort of sad. She didn't talk that much about it, but you could tell she minded.

I told Jonah about how Dad had said I could come out and live with him if I wanted.

"Are you going to?" he said nervously.

"I guess not. Mom and Suzu would miss me a lot. It's really dumb having two parents living that far apart."

"How come they do?"

"Well, Mom says the reason is after she got divorced she wanted to make a fresh start and go to a place she'd never been to before. And Dad says he had his business out there. And he thinks

New York is dirty and cold, and out there he can play tennis all year round."

"I don't think you'd like it that much out there," Jonah said.

"How do you know?"

"We went out once to visit my Aunt Selma, you know, that time we went to Disneyland, I told you. The kids out there are really strange. They talk about horoscopes all the time. That's the first thing they say to you practically. 'What's your sign?' " Jonah's going to be a scientist when he grows up so of course he thinks all that is dumb.

"Still, Dad has such a nice house. And there wouldn't be screaming and yelling like with Gabe and Mom."

"Yeah, but Gabe's gone away, so what're you worried about?"

"He might come back."

"Listen, Bernie, I'll tell you one thing. If your Dad has this new baby, there'll be *plenty* of yelling. You just don't know because you got Suzu when she was over all that. There'll be smelly diaper pails in the bathroom so you practically throw up when you go in there. And babies wreck anything they lay their hands on and people don't even stop them. They say, 'Oh, he can't help it, he's just a little baby.' They think it's cute or something."

"Yeah, well, I don't think I'll go to really *live* there," I said. He did have a lot of good points.

Jonah is very logical about things. "I might visit, though. Or I might call collect."

"Right, calling sounds like a much better idea."

Thanksgiving came. Usually that's when Grandma comes to stay with us, but she called up and said she couldn't this year. She said she had a boyfriend named Sol Lieberman, a lovely widower, and he wanted her to go to Puerto Rico with him for a week over Thanksgiving. "I'll come see you as soon as I get back," she said.

"You can't have a boyfriend, Grandma," I said. "You're too old."

"Nonsense!" Grandma said. "You're never too old."

"What does 'widower' mean?"

"It means his wife died."

"Does he want to marry you?"

"Sort of."

"Are you going to marry him?"

"Don't rush me, Bernie. We're just friends, that's all."

Mom said, "Let me talk to her, Bernie."

I gave her the phone and she said, "What's all this, Mother? No monkey business! You be careful!"

I went to listen in on the other extension. I heard Grandma say, "I can take care of myself, Becka. Don't worry about me."

"I *do* worry about you. You're going to find some other man who'll want you to wait on him hand and foot and then toss you out when the whim seizes him, just like Father."

"Becka, don't be so cynical."

"I'm being real*i*stic. You know the women in our family and their dealings with men. You know—"

"How's Gabe, speaking of—"

"Oh, he's fine."

"He went—" I started to say, but Mom broke in.

"Bern, put Suzu on, will you? Grandma would like to speak to her."

I went and got Suzu. The funny thing is, even though Suzu talks really well now, she hates to talk on the phone. She just holds the phone and breathes into it.

"Hi there, Suzu," Grandma said.

Suzu just sat there.

"Say hi," I told her.

"Are you there, honey? It's Grandma. I'm sorry I can't come for Thanksgiving, but I'll see you really soon. Thank you for that nice picture you did."

Mom said, "She's a little bit shy on the phone."

"I am *not* shy," Suzu said loudly, but she wouldn't say anything more.

After we'd all hung up, Mom said, "Oh, it's just as well. I'm not up to a big Thanksgiving this year."

"If Grandma gets married, maybe I can be her

bridesmaid," I said. "Then I'll be a bridesmaid twice in one year."

"If she gets married, I'll shoot her," Mom said grimly.

Suzu laughed.

"No, I mean it, Grandma doesn't know what end is up. She's so naïve, I don't even want to *think* about it."

"But maybe Sol Lieberman is very nice. Do you think he murdered his wife?"

"No! Lord, why should I think that?"

"Well, she said he was a—that word meaning someone whose wife died."

"No, she probably died of cancer or some illness."

"Will we have a turkey and everything this year even if Grandma doesn't come?"

"I guess. Do you want one? Do you really like it?"

"Umm . . . Yum!"

"Well, this year you're going to have to help me, Bern. If you want a turkey and all that, you help me make it."

"O.K., I will."

I always get excited around Thanksgiving because my birthday is the day after Christmas. That's not such a great time to have a birthday, but that's when I was born, so I can't help it.

Fooling Mrs. Mondale

One Saturday morning in December Suzu and I woke up early and it was snowing. It was the first snow of the winter. Suzu got all excited so we put on our coats to go out in the yard. "If there's more, we can make a snowman," I told her.

I called up Jonah. "It's snowing," I said.

"Great."

"Want to go sledding if there's enough?"

"Sure."

"O.K., I'll see you later."

When we came in, we were starving. I thought Mom would be up by then since it was ten o'clock, but she was still sleeping. I decided to make French toast. I know how. Mom says I can use the top of the stove, but not the oven if she's not up. Suzu ate around four slices! I guess I'm a pretty good cook. I think I'll write a cookbook after I finish about Mamie.

I went over and looked at Mom's calendar. I wanted to count how many days there were till my birthday. Today, the third, was circled in red. It said: *Mrs. Mondale, 11:45.* Mrs. Mondale is that lady from the AAA—the Asian Adoption Agency—which is where we got Suzu. I looked at the clock. It was eleven thirty. I thought maybe I should wake up Mom because she didn't know what time it was. I said to Suzu, "Let's wake up Mommy."

Suzu ran into the bedroom and jumped on the bed. Mom was buried way under the covers. Suzu went and sat on her head.

"Oh, God," Mom said. "It must be nighttime, it's so dark out."

"It's snowing!" I said. "The first snow."

"It's freezing, *brr.*"

"Mom?"

"What?"

"Mrs. Mondale is coming at eleven forty-five and it's eleven thirty."

Mom stared at me. She looked like I said someone was going to put her in jail. "No!" she said.

"It's on your calendar."

"It can't be. Oh, no!"

"Should I bring you your calendar?"

Suddenly Mom started to cry. Suzu looked at her curiously.

"What's wrong?" I said.

"But—I'm not even up yet! The house! It's a wreck. Oh, Jesus, what'll I do?"

"Will she take Suzu away?"

"Honey, listen," Mom said, "don't tell her about Gabe, O.K.? Just say he's away on a trip, if she asks. If she doesn't ask, don't say anything. I'll get dressed, but if she comes before I'm ready, just say I'll be right there. Will you?"

"Sure," I said. "We had breakfast already. I made French toast."

"Bern, you're the best that money can buy. Really."

Mom leaped out of bed and I took Suzu inside. It was lucky we did wake Mom up because about three seconds later the doorbell rang and it was Mrs. Mondale.

"You must be Bernadette and—this must be Suzu?" she said.

"Can I hang up your coat?" I said. Her coat was really heavy—it was like carrying a person. It was lined with fur.

"That's Grandma," Suzu whispered.

"No, it's not," I whispered back.

"Well, I *am* a grandma, actually," Mrs. Mondale said. She wasn't half as pretty as our grandma. "But not *your* grandma. My name is Mrs. Mondale."

"Grandma Monday?" Suzu said.

Boy, she was getting everything all mixed up.

I hope Mrs. Mondale doesn't take her away. "Suzu is all excited from the snow," I said.

"Bernie will make a snowman," Suzu said. "She knows how."

"I'll bet she does," Mrs. Mondale said. "Well, where are your mother and father, Bernadette? I smell something good cooking for breakfast."

"It's French toast," I said. "Would you like some? There's an extra piece."

"Oh, thank you, maybe I will, just a *tiny* piece. I'm really on a diet, but it smells so awfully good. You said your parents—"

"Daddy gone," Suzu said.

"Yeah, he—he had some work this morning. Mom will be out in a second, though."

"Mommy sleeping," Suzu said.

"No, she's *not!* You saw her get up. Suzu isn't too sure about time yet," I said quickly.

"Well, she seems to be doing very nicely. I'm amazed at her speech."

"She knows the alphabet," I said.

Suddenly Suzu started singing in this very loud voice, "ABCDEFG . . ." She sang to the end, but when she came to, "Now I know my ABC" she stopped. "Don't know what comes next," she said.

"Next comes, 'Tell me what you think of me,'" I said.

"I do it again," Suzu said.

"You did it very nicely," Mrs. Mondale said.

"No, I forgot," Suzu said and she sang it all through again.

"Well, that's really *very nice*," said Mrs. Mondale. "I bet it helps to have a big sister like Bernadette." She had finished her French toast. "What class are you in at school, Suzu?"

"Zachary's," Suzu said.

"He's her friend," I said. "Really, she's in kindergarten."

"I bet you have a lot of friends," Mrs. Mondale said.

Suzu didn't say anything.

"She likes Sarah and Tommy," I said. "They come to her house."

"I a boy," Suzu said suddenly.

"Are you?" Mrs. Mondale looked surprised. "You look like a nice little girl to me."

"She just likes to say that," I said. "She doesn't like to wear dresses."

Mrs. Mondale just kept smiling as though she wasn't sure what to say next. I said, "You can see our room if you like. It's not that straightened up, though."

"Oh, well, it looks very lived in," Mrs. Mondale said when she came in.

I wonder why she said that. Of *course* it was lived in!

Suzu got out her Gray Mouse and Elephant and brought them to Mrs. Mondale. "Those are her favorites," I said.

"Oh . . . and this poor little mouse has a Band-Aid, I see," Mrs. Mondale said.

"He bit him," Suzu said.

81

"The elephant?"

"He hates him, he put him in jail," Suzu said.

"That's too bad, isn't it? I hope they manage to fox up their quarrel, I mean fix up their quarrel."

I couldn't help laughing, the way she said fox up their quarrel. But then I thought that might not be polite so I pulled my cheeks in and tried to think of something sad.

Suzu took the elephant and began banging it against the mouse. "Bang! Bang!" she said. To Mrs. Mondale she said, "He bit him. See!" She pointed to the Band-Aid.

"The elephant bit the mouse?"

Suzu nodded.

"Well, I'm sorry to hear that. It's not nice for big people to bite little people. In fact, I guess biting is never a very good way to settle quarrels."

Suzu went off in the corner playing with something.

"Bernadette, did you say your mother was up? I might just—"

"Oh, yeah, she'll be out in one second," I said. Then I remembered I said that around ten minutes earlier. I went and knocked on Mom's door. "Mom!"

Mom came out. She took Mrs. Mondale's hand. "Hi, I'm so sorry I overslept."

"She ate a piece of French toast," I said.

"Bernie's a pretty good cook, isn't she?" Mom said.

82

"Splendid."

"Did you show Mrs. Mondale your notebook, Bern?"

"What notebook is that?"

"Oh, Bernie's been writing all these stories."

"I'd love to see them," Mrs. Mondale said.

She sat on the couch looking at "Mamie and the Hebrew War." I didn't bring them all down. Mom sat watching her. She looked nervous and kept biting her nails. Mrs. Mondale looked up. "This is a very sad story, isn't it, Bernadette?"

"Yeah, well, you have to write sad things sometimes," I said. "Because life is sad."

"True, true. What happened to Mamie's parents? You don't mention them."

"She lost them. It's a war."

"*Lost* them?"

"Yeah, that's what happens in a war." You could tell she didn't know much about it.

"And these—these rough women? Who are they?"

"They're imaginary."

"I see. They don't seem like very pleasant individuals. I hope I don't run into them on a dark night."

I didn't say anything. I *told* her it was imaginary! So, why should she run into them on a dark night? Grown-ups are strange.

Mrs. Mondale smiled at Mom. "Well, Bernadette certainly has a lively imagination, doesn't she? I admire creative people very much myself."

"My husband is very creative," Mom said, biting her nails. "He had a show of his sculpture over at the college. This is the catalogue."

"Fascinating," Mrs. Mondale said, not really looking at it. She looked outside. "Well, I'd love to stay longer, but that sky looks a little ominous. I think I'd better get off while the roads are still manageable."

"It was so nice of you to come," Mom said. Her face had this funny expression, like she was afraid Mrs. Mondale was mad at her.

"I enjoyed it. Thank you for that delicious French toast, Bernadette. I think you're going to make some man very happy some day with that fine cooking."

"I'm not getting married," I said. "I'm going to be a bachelor."

"You mean a spinster?"

"I don't know."

"I think it's a little soon to be deciding all that, Bernie," Mom said, kind of glaring at me.

"No, it's not! I'm eleven years old!"

Mom and Mrs. Mondale both smiled.

Suzu came out. "I'm glad to see you're getting along so nicely, Suzu," Mrs. Mondale said. "And I'm especially pleased to have made the acquaintance of that elephant and mouse of yours."

"You take me away?" Suzu demanded.

"Take you *away?*"

"Bernie said you take me away, put me back in Vietnam."

"I did *not!*"

"Yes, you did!"

"No, of course, nothing like that will take place," Mrs. Mondale said, startled. She put on her heavy coat. "Good-by, everyone."

As soon as she had left, I went over and yelled at Suzu. "Boy, you're really *dumb!* Why'd you say that? Now she might *really* take you away!"

Suzu began to cry.

Mom went over and hugged her. "Bernie, for Christ's sake!" she said. "Scaring Suzu like that! You're eleven years old and you act like a two year old at times. Suzu is going nowhere. She's staying right here with us."

"You're the one who said it," I said. "It's not *my* fault."

"O.K., let's forget about whose fault it is. The point is, this is Suzu's home. This is where she belongs."

Suzu was still sniffling a little. She peeked at me from inside Mom's arms. "Come on, don't cry, Suzu," I said. "You can play with my Wacky Packs. Wasn't I good, Mom?"

"You were great, Bern, you were supreme." She went in to pour a cup of coffee. Suzu ran in to get the Wackies. "But what was that story you showed her? That sounded pretty grim."

"It isn't grim. It's about this little girl."

Mom sighed. "Well, anyhow, it all worked out, that's what counts."

"Aren't you glad I didn't tell her about Gabe being gone?"

"I'm more than glad."

"And wasn't it good I woke you up?"

"It was fantastic."

"You shouldn't have bit your nails," I said. "You could tell you were nervous."

"Bern, luckily for all of us, I don't think everyone is quite as sharp-eyed as you." She looked at her nails. "But you're right. I ought to stop biting them."

"I used to bite my toenails," I said. "But I can't reach them anymore."

Christmas at Jonah's

"Girls, be good, O.K.?" Mom said.

"We always are," I said.

"Well, extra special." She hugged and kissed us and then she rode off in the car.

It was the day before Christmas. We were staying at Jonah's house for a few days. Mom had to go away for her job. Usually she said she would have said something like she just couldn't because it's Suzu's first Christmas with us and my birthday, but now that Gabe is gone, she said she can't afford to do anything that might make the people at her job mad at her. Because then they might fire her and we wouldn't have any money.

I don't mind being with Jonah's family except for one thing. They're Jewish like us only they celebrate Chanukah instead, which means they don't have a Christmas tree. After Mom left, Jonah's mother said we should all go sledding.

"It's too cold," Jonah's father said.

"Cold! It's twenty-nine degrees."

"I'm going to sit by the fire and spin," said Jonah's father. He's a big tall fat man with a beard.

"I want to too," Jonah said.

"Come on, gang," Jonah's mother said. "You need exercise! You need fresh air!" Jonah's mother likes sports a lot. In the summer she plays tennis and swims and in the winter she skis and ice skates. She has red cheeks and a round nose. Her name is Gertrude, but Jonah's father calls her Potter.

It was fun sledding. Suzu screamed every time she went down, but in an excited way. When we got to the bottom, she always said, "Again!" Jonah's mother went down with Zachary sitting in front of her.

I pulled Jonah up the hill.

"Jonah! What *is* this? Why is Bernie pulling you?"

"He's tired," I said.

"What? Look, get off! He weighs over a hundred pounds and you're pulling him? That's ridiculous!"

"I don't mind," I said.

"Well, I do. Jonah needs the exercise more than any of us if he wants to work some of that fat off his tushy."

Jonah looked really angry at his mother. That was a mean thing to say. "I don't mind pulling you," I whispered.

"No, it's O.K.," he said. He got up slowly. "We went to the doctor and I weighed four pounds more. That's why she's mad."

"I don't mind if you're fat," I said.

"You have to say that."

"Why?"

"Because you're my best friend. You want to cheer me up."

"No, I don't. Anyway, your father is fat."

"I know. He thinks the whole thing is silly."

Suzu thinks Jonah's father is Santa Claus. I guess she never had Christmas before. "Where your sack?" she said when we were back in the house.

"Oh, I have that stored away," Jonah's father said. "With my sled and reindeer and all my gear."

"Want to *see* gear," Suzu said.

"Yeah, Santa, where's your reindeer?" I asked.

"Oh, my reindeer are very shy," he said. "Very shy, delicate creatures. They would panic at the sight of all these healthy, robust boys and girls."

"I'm shy," Suzu said.

"No, you're not. You don't even know what that *means*," I said.

"Supper in ten minutes!" called Jonah's mother.

I like Jonah's mother, even though she's mean to Jonah about being fat. She cooks things like

89

French fries for supper, which Mom says are too rich, and she even had cupcakes for dessert, even though it wasn't anyone's birthday. Before supper I tried to tell Suzu about getting divorced because she might wonder about Gabe not coming back. "It's when your daddy goes away," I said. Then I thought she might get that mixed up with Vietnam and her daddy going away there.

"Mommy go away too?" she said.

"No . . . just your Daddy."

"Bernie go away?"

"No! *I* can't go away! I'm just a child."

"*I* go away?"

"No!" Oh, boy, little kids really don't understand anything!

"We get new daddy?"

"No! You just get rid of the old one, dumbhead! You don't get a new one. At least not right away."

"Want new daddy," Suzu said.

"Well, she won't bring one, because that's not how it goes."

After supper Suzu got into her feet pajamas. She won't wear nightgowns, just pajamas with feet. She went and sat on Jonah's father's lap. "Daddy in your sack?" she said.

"A daddy in my sack, a daddy in my sack. No, I don't believe so . . . why?"

"Want new daddy for Christmas. We give away old one."

"We didn't give away our old one," I said. To

Jonah's mother and father I said, "She doesn't understand about getting divorced."

Suzu was stroking Jonah's father's beard. "Beard talk," she said.

"This beard says, 'Who is this charming young lady stroking me? She's tickling me,' he says."

Suzu laughed. "Talk more!"

"She wants everything to talk," I said.

"Daddy, I want to sit in your lap!" Zachary said.

"Come here, Suzu . . . it's Zachary's turn now," I told her.

I went into the bathroom to get ready for bed. It was a little strange not having a Christmas tree and no place to hang up stockings, but it was exciting to be sleeping at Jonah's house. We were sleeping on sleeping bags on the floor in Jonah and Zachary's room. Zachary still doesn't talk that much but he follows Jonah around a lot.

When I came back, Suzu was saying to Jonah's father, "You Santa?"

"You can't be Santa Claus," I said, "because you're Jewish."

"Bernie, you have a precise and logical mind," Jonah's father said. "You will go far."

After we had tucked into our sleeping bags, Suzu whispered to me, "Want Jonah's daddy for my daddy."

"Well, he can't be your daddy because he's married already. He has his own children."

"Why?"

"Because he just can't," I said impatiently. "You can't marry two people."

"Why?"

"Because you just can't. If you do, they put you in jail."

"Jonah's daddy in jail?"

"No! Oh, it's too complicated to explain. Mom isn't even in love with him."

"*I* love him," Suzu said.

"Well, you better stop."

"He take me to the North Pole."

"He's just teasing you. He's not *really* Santa Claus."

"He has reindeer."

"He's just making that up."

But in the morning when Suzu found all her presents in the living room, she said to me, "He *is* Santa Claus! See!" To Jonah's father she said, "Where your reindeer?"

"Oh, they're resting peacefully after their long night's work."

The trouble was it got warm on Christmas and all the snow melted. We played hide and seek for a while, but Suzu doesn't know how to hide in good places. Also, she counts in a funny way. She says, "One, two, three, four, five, eight, ten, eleventeen, sixteen, seventeen, twenty!" Then, if she finds you in some good place—usually you have to yell out to her what room you're in or she'd *never* find you!—she wants to hide there herself for the next time and of course you know where she is. Oh, well. Zachary isn't that good either. He just likes to hide, he never even wants to be It.

For my birthday the next day I got a really great magic set. Jonah and I decided that when it gets warm, we'll give a carnival and we can do magic tricks. We can charge admission and have refreshments and everything.

It was a nice day for my birthday. The sun came out and Jonah and I went to Central Park to play. We went to this place near the playground that we used to call Magic Rock. Of course, it's not really magic. It's just this big white rock you can sit on. But when we were little, we used to go there and pretend that if you sat on the rock, you could cast magic spells. We pretended there was this witch that was wicked and could make us do things. It was really a witch candle. Then she lost her wick, so she couldn't be wicked anymore. No one but Jonah and I know about Magic Rock because it's a secret. If either of us tells, the witch could put a spell on us. I'll never tell, not even if someone says they'll kill me if I don't. Sometimes Jonah hides candy there in a tin box and he comes out to eat it without his mother knowing. Like from parties. He doesn't steal it, it's his candy, only if he saved it in the house, she might take it away.

We had some peanut brittle and sour balls.

"I hope Mom doesn't lose her job," I said.

"She won't," Jonah said.

"If she did," I said, "we might be really poor. And we might have to move away."

"Will you put newspapers in your shoes?"

There was this movie Jonah and I saw where poor people had to put newspapers in their shoes. Also, the pig had to live in the house with them. I hope that doesn't happen to us. Of course, we don't have a pig yet.

"If your mother ever says you have to move away, you come here and I'll hide you," Jonah said.

"Where?"

"In my closet."

"Will you bring me food at night?"

"Sure. Only I can't hide Suzu too. She'd make too much noise."

I felt better that Jonah would hide me. Anyway, maybe we won't move *or* be poor.

When we came in the house, Jonah's mother rushed over and said, "Mazel tov, Bernie. You have a little brother."

"I do?"

"Yes, your father sent a telegram. I didn't know Becka had told him you'd be here."

"She didn't . . . I did."

"His name is Jacob Nguyen Sato. He was born right on your birthday!"

"Hey, that's great," Jonah said. "Did you plan that?"

I shook my head.

"It's really an amazing coincidence," Jonah's mother said.

"This calls for a celebration," Jonah's father said.

"Mommy had baby?" Suzu said.

"No! How could she? She's not even pregnant!"

"I have brother?" Suzu said.

"No, *I* do," I said. "You don't have anything."

"She's an aunt," Jonah said.

"No, she isn't. How could she be an aunt?"

"Well, what does this make me?" Jonah said.

"It makes you a person who is happy that his friend has a baby brother," Jonah's mother said. "This is getting too confusing. I'm getting a headache."

"I think this makes me an uncle," Jonah said.

"I think this makes me very hungry," Jonah's father said. "Where is this famous lunch I have heard tell about?"

"This famous lunch is going to be served in one second," Jonah's mother said.

After lunch I asked Jonah's father if I could use his typewriter. I wanted to start my cookbook. I dedicated it to Suzu and Jacob. Jonah's father's typewriter is different from Mom's. It's electric and that means if you just touch the keys lightly it types. You don't have to bang on it. I guess it costs a lot of money. I wish I could have one.

"Bernie, I think Jonah would like to play with

you," Jonah's father said after I'd been typing awhile.

"O.K., I'm just finishing."

"What are you working on?"

"It's a cookbook. Do you want to see it? It's not finished yet, of course. I'm doing desserts first."

He looked at it. "Hmm . . . Coffee Relaxedness sounds like something I could use right now, along with a big helping of Animal Bounders Fudge. Will you make me some?"

"Sometime," I said. "But I don't have time now. If you like those recipes, you might want to buy my book when it comes out."

"I most certainly will. I hope I'll get an autographed copy."

The next day Mom was coming to pick us up. I kept thinking about her all day. Even though Jonah's parents are nice, I missed her. I guess I'm sort of old to be like that, but I did. When we heard the doorbell ring twice, we knew it was Mom. She came into the house. Suzu was waving this Dapper Dan doll she got. "Look!"

"Oh, goodness, look at that beautiful doll," Mom said. We were both hugging her.

"Santa Claus," Suzu said, pointing to Jonah's father.

"Hmm, I always suspected something with that beard," Mom said. "Hi, Fletcher! Hi, Gert!"

"Hi yourself," said Jonah's father. "How'd it go?"

"Pretty good."

We told Mom about Jacob Nguyen. She hadn't heard because she was away on her job.

"Isn't that great?" I said.

"Let's call them tonight," Mom said.

On the way home Suzu said, "No more Daddy?"

"What?"

"She means getting divorced," I said. "I told her about it."

"Bernie!"

"What's wrong? She had to know."

Mom sighed. "Bern, it's complicated. You don't just go in and clap your hands and, bingo, you're divorced. It takes a long time."

"*How* long?"

"It depends. Hey, I got a raise."

"Hurray!"

"Only, listen, kid, it means we'll all have to buckle down. Things will be harder all around. I'll be working later. We'll have to have Cynthia more."

"O.K." I stared out the window. There still wasn't much snow. "But you better not do it again," I said.

"What?"

"Get married. Because all you do is get divorced."

"Oh, honey, that's cruel."

"It's true."

"That's not *all* I do. Look, I loved Gabe, I loved Dad at the time. . . ."

"So, why did you divorce them?"

"Hon, you're too young to understand everything."

"You always say that."

"No, I don't. Lots of things you do understand, just not everything. Be a child, Bern! Really, later you'll wish you had—"

"Taken advantage of it." I finished the sentence for her.

She laughed. "I doubt I'll marry again, Bern . . . not for a long, long time, if ever. So I wouldn't worry about it."

I told her I wouldn't.

Secrets

Things are different now that Mom has her raise. Sometimes when she comes home from work, it's seven. I help Cynthia make supper for Suzu. We don't have anything fancy, just peanut-butter-and-jelly sandwiches or hot dogs. Suzu likes hot dogs with mustard and sauerkraut on a roll, but she doesn't eat the roll. Then she has strawberry milk in her snorkel cup. She doesn't usually have dessert. Mom says Suzu doesn't have a sweet tooth and that's good because it means she won't get so many cavities.

Sometimes Suzu is a big pest if I have home-work to do. She just sits right outside the study and yells, "Bernie, come out!" Cynthia keeps trying to say, "Wouldn't you like me to read you a nice book, Suzu?" Suzu says, "No! Bernie read to me!" I just tell Suzu I'm doing homework. Actually, I'm working on my cookbook. I've decided to have a section on breakfast food because that's when kids are up and parents are usually asleep, so it's a good time for kids to make their own food. I've decided to call my cookbook *The Divorced Child's Cookbook* because children who come from a home with a divorce in it have to help out more with things like cooking. They would like a book like mine.

When Grandma heard about Mom divorcing Gabe, she said she would come right away to help us out. Mom said we didn't need any help, we were doing just fine. Grandma said don't be silly, she would come anyway, and Mom said if she was so set to come, why didn't she come in March, when the play I wrote was being put on in school. Grandma said she would just love to.

I guess you would like to know about my play. It's about African animals because that's what we studied this year in school—Africa. It's called, "Hi, Lunch!" because that's what the Panther (Jonah) says to the Gazelle when he sees him. You see, he thinks he can eat him for lunch, but the Gazelle gets away. I'm the Mother Elephant.

Grandma loved the play. She sat in the first row. I was glad, because Mom had to work that night and if Grandma hadn't come, I wouldn't have had anyone from my family. "Author! Author!" Grandma yelled. She said that's what you're supposed to do so the person who wrote the play will come out and bow.

"I wish school had been like this in my day," Grandma said.

"I'm sorry about this business with Gabe," Grandma said the next afternoon when we were playing Careers. "These things are always hardest on the children. I've always said that."

"I'm not sorry. I hope he never comes back," I said.

"Well, people have faults, Bernie. You mustn't judge them too harshly."

I wondered if Grandma knew all the bad things about Gabe. "He used bad words," I said. "And he yelled. At Mom *and* us."

Grandma sighed.

"We'll manage O.K., Grandma." There's one thing I didn't tell Grandma. That's that I wrote to Francesca. See, I have her address because I once copied it into my address book. I decided to write and ask her if she knew where Gabe was because Mom says she doesn't. She hasn't answered yet, but maybe she will and then we can correspond with each other. I like to correspond with people.

Dad said he was glad Gabe had left. I called him once collect to talk about his baby. He said again how much he hoped we would all come out and visit.

I wish Dad would move to New York. He says

he would give anything to, but right now it just doesn't seem possible. Sometimes I think of doing what he said, going out there to live all year round. But Suzu would practically kill herself and Mom would be really mad. So I guess I won't. If I were magic, I would make Dad and Peggy get divorced and Mom and Dad get married again and Dad would move here. Peggy could have the baby if she wanted. Then we'd be a regular family with two children just like Jonah's. The trouble is, I'm not magic.

Grandma was looking worried. She bit the end of her card. "Becka needs a man around. She's so tense these days. She must have lost ten pounds! She's all skin and bones. And she flies off the handle so easily."

"That's just her personality. Gabe flew off *his* handle too."

"If she could only find the right man!"

"Maybe she could find one of those people like you did. I forget what they're called."

Grandma looked startled. "What do you mean?"

"You know, that person whose wife had died."

"Oh, Sol. A widower, you mean?"

"Yeah, a lovely widower. Maybe she could use one of those."

"Sol is such a marvelous person, Bernie. I hope some day soon you and he will meet. He's read some of your stories and he couldn't get over them. Never heard of such a talented child, he said. And he has eleven grandchildren, mind you!"

"Are you going to marry him?"

Grandma didn't say anything for a long, long time. Then she said, "Do you swear on a million bibles not to breathe a word to your mother?"

"I swear," I said. I was really excited.

"We *are* married," Grandma whispered. She turned pink.

"You are?" I hugged her.

"Promise me, though, Bernie. Because you know your mother. She'll *kill* me if she finds out."

"She won't *kill* you!" I laughed.

"She'll be *very, very* angry. And if you'd only all meet him. Let me show you his picture." She went to her handbag and showed me a photo. He was tan with white hair and a moustache. "Now I never liked handsome men; they made me nervous. Too full of themselves, I always said. And here I am at sixty-two marrying a man handsome enough to be a movie star. And you never *saw* anyone less vain. Not a vain bone in his body, never even *looks* in the mirror. Why, when his birthday came around and I bought him these two shirts, perfectly ordinary shirts, nice ones though, nice colors, he just looked at them and said, 'Oh, these are too good, Margot.'"

"He sounds nice," I said.

"It's not just a matter of nice, Bernie. Lots of people are nice. It's—well, look at all the interests he has! That's what impresses me. Your grandfather when he retired—why, he almost drove me loony creeping around the kitchen in his slippers all the time, sneaking up on me. Just didn't know what in God's name to do with himself. Whereas Sol! Why, the day's not full enough for him to get done all he'd like to do. It's an inspiration to me, I can tell you. He's a weaver."

"A weaver?"

"Oh, I wish I'd brought that photo of the rug he wove for my living room, Bernie. I couldn't put it on the floor. I couldn't bear it. I said to him, 'Sol, you can't expect me to put that right on the floor where people will *step* all over it! It's a work of *art!*' It was! It had the most beautiful colors, Bernie. I've never seen anything like that in my life. He wants to make one for you as soon as you decide what colors you'd like. He says he feels like he knows you already, I talk so much about you."

"Did he used to be a weaver before?"

"No! That's what's so striking, to *me*, anyway. He was a lawyer. Just a regular office job, but he had all these interests, you see. He never was like your grandfather—just into the office, back home, grind, grind, grind. No, Sol plays the cello, he does yoga. Bernie, I know it sounds funny to say this, but if there is a God, I really do thank him for the chance to meet someone like Sol in my lifetime."

"Mom says she doesn't believe in God."

"Well, I don't either, *really*. But there are times

when you want to thank someone. Because how do you explain it otherwise? I want to tell you we almost *didn't* meet. It was such a fluke. I wasn't even supposed to go into the store that day. I just thought—well, I'll drop by, maybe they need me. I usually go in Monday, Thursday, and Saturday, one to seven. But sometimes they get rushed so I nip in to help out. Well, sure, they said, we could use you, Margot—they call me by my first name, but I don't mind. Don't tell your mother or she might think it's lack of respect. It's *not!* So, there I was, not in the store more than five minutes when who should walk in but this distinguished-looking man with a moustache asking for some organic peanut butter. His grandchild was coming for the weekend, you see. Of course I didn't know that then! So we started talking and right away we hit it off. It's a funny thing. Some people, you know them twenty, thirty years and you never say a word of any consequence. But with Sol after ten minutes we felt like we'd known each other forever! It was uncanny! It wasn't just me. He felt that way too. And just think. What if I hadn't decided to go in that day? When I think of that, I just feel *dark* inside."

"But you did go."

"I did, thank the good lord or whoever arranges such things. I don't care *who* arranges them, but I thank that person or thing."

"Do you believe that when you die, you go to heaven?" I asked.

"No! You know, Bernie, your grandfather was always after me to go to synagogue. Not that he believed one whit more than I did, mind you, but he always said it was the proper thing to do. 'You go, then,' I'd say. *I* never went. He used to take your mother till she was old enough to say No, and the two of them would come back, hand in hand. But I never went."

"I think I might even believe in God," I said.

"Well, you do as you like, Bernie. That's the main thing. If you believe, fine. If you don't, don't give a hang what the neighbors think. Now that's just what Sol says. Like with his weaving. He says his daughter-in-law, the one who lives in Minneapolis, she says what will people *think:* a grown man, weaving? He says, '*I* don't care, let them think what they like. They—' "

Just then the door opened. Grandma winked at me and whispered, "Remember our secret?"

I grinned. "Don't worry. I'm good at keeping secrets."

Funny Business

The last day Grandma stayed was this great day. It was seventy-five degrees and only March! Suzu and I got up early, at six, and played outside in the yard. One thing I love to do is squish with bare feet in the mud. I just love the feeling when the mud goes oozing up through my toes. And I love digging for worms. I don't like to fish much, but I love just getting worms and putting them in cans. Luckily, I saved this Chock Full o' Nuts coffee can so Suzu and I made it into a worm house and we pretended it was a castle and there was a queen worm and a king worm. The thing with worms is that it's hard to tell them apart, but that doesn't really matter.

"Show worms to Grandma?" Suzu said.

"No, we'll bring her outside. Hey, quick! We

better hurry. We're bringing her breakfast in bed, remember?"

"Why?"

"Because it's her birthday."

"Cake?"

"No, grown-ups don't . . . But this is a surprise and you have to help."

I got out the biggest tray and we really made a wonderful breakfast for Grandma: one soft-boiled egg, two pieces of toast with margarine, a salt shaker and pepper grinder, a cinnamon-and-sugar shaker on the side, and one cup of instant coffee. I don't know how to make regular coffee, but instant is easy—you just boil water.

"Now be very very quiet," I said. "It has to be a surprise."

We tiptoed down the hall. Mom was still sleeping. I was carrying the tray. "Now!" I whispered to Suzu.

She threw open the door and ran into Grandma's room yelling, "Happy birthday!"

Grandma was just sitting up in bed reading. I had thought she might be asleep. "Goodness! What is this? Why you girls must have gotten up at the crack of dawn to do all this work!"

"We always get up at the crack of dawn," I said.

"We make house for worms," Suzu said.

Grandma looked surprised, but I said, "It's outside. You can see it later." I put the tray down near Grandma. "First you have to look at the card."

Grandma opened the card I had made for her. On the front side it said in big letters, "You're sixty-three!" and inside it said, "Go on and on." "Why, Bernie," Grandma said. "I think that's one of the nicest things anyone has ever said to me. I certainly will try to go on and on. Come here and let me kiss and squeeze both of you."

Suzu was tucked in next to Grandma. "I want breakfast too," she said.

"Suzu, you get out! That's for Grandma. It's not *your* birthday."

"Yes," Suzu said. "My birthday too."

"Oh, I can spare a bit of toast," Grandma said. "Look at how you've fixed the whole thing up. I can't get over it. Wait till I tell Sol about this."

I made a face at Grandma, meaning she shouldn't tell Suzu about Sol because Suzu can't keep a secret. She smiled back.

Later we showed Grandma our worm house and then Mom had to drive her to the airport. "Now remember! No excuses this time! You're all coming out to see me this summer. Why don't you leave them with me, Becka? You look like you need a nice, long rest."

Mom didn't say anything.

"Sol and I—I'll take perfectly good care of them. And you can get yourself back on your feet again."

"I *am* back on my feet!" Mom said angrily.

"Oh, of course you are, darling. You're managing wonderfully. I just thought—"

After Grandma got on her plane, Mom said, "There's some funny business going on with Grandma and that man. I just *know* it."

"Sol?"

"I don't like the looks of it a bit," Mom said. "Love among the senior citizens!" She snorted.

"I love Grandma," I said.

"Well, we all love her," Mom said. "That's why we're worried. Because she has no more sense of how to handle herself around men than a newborn baby."

"Grandma is baby?" Suzu said.

"Get back on my feet!" Mom snorted again. "Let *her* stay on *hers,* I say!"

A Telegram from Dad

One day in April we got a telegram. Usually on TV that means someone has died. But Mom didn't look that sad. "Hmm . . . strange," she said.

"Let me see it!" I yelled, jumping up and down.

"Let me see it!" Suzu said. What good would it do for her to see it? She can't even read! She just likes to copy me.

I read it. It said: PEGGY HAS RECEIVED OBSCENE AMOUNT OF MONEY FOR SCRIPT STOP ENCLOSED THREE TICKETS TO CAL STOP CALL US COLLECT STOP LOVE FUMIO.

"What does an obscene amount of money mean?" I said.

"Oh, it's hard to explain, Bern," Mom said. "It means a lot of money."

"Are they rich? Are they millionaires? Are they trillionaires?"

"No, honey, calm down. They just have some extra money and they want us all to go visit them."

"Now?"

"Whenever we want."

I didn't say anything. I knew Mom would never do it after what she had said about Peggy before.

"So, what do you think?" Mom said.

"What do you mean?"

"Should we go?" said Mom.

"But you hate Peggy," I said.

"I don't hate Peggy," Mom said. "How can I? I never met her."

"But that time I went to Boston and I said I might go out there, you got really mad."

"Bernie, listen. First of all, you know how upset I was then with Gabe just taking off like that, not knowing what was going to happen. And I was jealous of Dad and Peggy, let's face it."

"Aren't you still jealous?"

"No. I was jealous partly because I was afraid we couldn't manage on our own. But I think we're doing pretty well, don't you? Anyhow, remember, kid, how you pulled that number about going out to live there with them. You scared me silly!"

"I never said I was going to live there *all* the time."

"No, but it—well, you don't know, Bern, but if a father remarries and his former wife doesn't or is divorced again, he can go to court and get custody. You know, saying the child would be happier in a normal home. Which means he can just take the child away and there isn't anything the mother can do."

"But Dad wouldn't do that."

"At the time I didn't know . . . I thought he might."

"You mean kidnap me?"

"Not kidnap. You'd have gone out there for a visit and never come back. That's legal. It's not called kidnaping, it's called getting custody."

"But it didn't happen."

"I know! Look, that's what I'm saying. But I once knew someone it *did* happen to, so maybe I was overly scared. No, you're right, I don't think Dad would do that. I did kind of let my fears run away with me." She looked happier. "I'm sort of curious to meet Peggy and see the baby."

"So we're going?" I could hardly believe it.

"I'll call them and we'll talk about it."

"I know how to call them. I can call collect," I said. Then I stopped because I wasn't supposed to tell Mom I was calling Dad. But Mom didn't notice or must have figured I had just learned in school because she didn't say anything.

That night, when she came to tuck us in, she said, "Well, it's all worked out. Dad and Peggy have some friends who are going away and we can take their house. I'll have a two-week vacation and I'll take it then, in July."

"But what if you lose your job?"

"Honey, listen. Now this is my fault. I've gotten you too worried about all these things. Nothing is absolutely secure, but I'm good at my job, they like me, and even if they didn't, I could go out and get another job. So don't worry about that. In fact, just plain don't worry! We're going to have a wonderful vacation and lie in the sun and get fat and tan and be as lazy as can be."

I guess I am excited except for this one thing. Wouldn't you know—this is the one year Jonah *isn't* going to camp. It's funny. What happened is he started to grow and he got much thinner. His mother thinks he's eating less, but really he's eating more only he's growing so fast you can't tell. So she figured he didn't have to go to that camp anymore.

"You're the luckiest person I know," Jonah said, when I told him. "You go to all these great places! We never even go *anywhere*."

I tried to look at it his way. "Dad and Peggy live in a dome. It's this special kind of house that—"

"I know! You told me." But he still looked mad.

I guess I felt like saying to Jonah that he was lucky in one way, that his family stayed together and weren't always getting new fathers and then getting rid of them. But I know he doesn't even think of that as something especially good so I didn't say anything.

Usually I'm excited at the end of school because we have assembly and move to the next class. Each class in turn walks under the arch and everyone, all the parents and stuff in the audience, claps. Sometimes the little kids, the ones in nursery school and kindergarten, wave at their grown-ups. Suzu did. Mom wanted her to wear a dress for assembly, but Suzu said No. She just wore her vegetable shirt, which has onions and peppers and celery on it, and a pair of shorts and white kneesocks and her baseball sneakers. She wanted to wear her baseball hat, but Mom said No, she was putting her foot down.

It was a pretty exciting day. Our class did only a little skit, not a real play. I was just in the chorus and had to sing. Jonah played the grandfather and he talked in this really deep voice. Except once he forgot his lines and I whispered them to him. I guess he was nervous.

As soon as school was over, I began thinking about going to California. I kept crossing the days off on the calendar. That seemed to make the time go faster.

The day we were leaving, Mom kept running around saying, "I know I forgot something. What did I forget? Bern, think! What would I have been likely to forget?"

"Your head," I said and laughed.

"Thanks loads."

Suzu was in our room singing this song, "Cockadoodledoo, my dame has lost her shoe."

"Cockadoodle dat, my dame has lost her hat," I said.

"Bernie, Suzu, we're leaving in five minutes," Mom called. "Are you all ready?"

"Cockadoodle wig, my dame has lost her pig," I said. I was in this sort of silly mood.

"That's a great song, but pay attention, kids! Have you picked the toy you want to take?"

"Want to take Mousie and Snoopy and Polar Bear and Ernie and—" Suzu started to say.

"Hon, I said *one* toy. We're flying and we can't bring a lot of stuff."

"Cockadoodle woomio, my dame has lost her Fumio," I said.

"Bernie, come on. Be of some help. Are you all set?"

"I don't see why I can't bring my typewriter," I said, making a face.

"Hon, it's heavy! And it's old. And I'm sure they have one. And what's even more important, this is a vacation. And a vacation means playing, not working. It means leaving behind all your usual cares and just plain having fun."

"But my typing *is* fun," I said. Mom always thinks my typing is work. It's funny that I've told her nine million times it isn't work and she still says the same thing.

116

When we were at the airport, Suzu said, "That's our plane?"

"Yeah, isn't it great?"

"I fly plane!" Suzu said.

Mom got a whole jumbo bag of Dubble-Bubble Gum because she said it would help keep our ears from clogging. We got three seats together, Suzu on the aisle and Mom in the middle. I was glad Suzu didn't want the window because then I'd have had to give it to her and I like looking out. Mom touched my arm and her hand was freezing cold. I jumped.

"How come your hands are like that?"

"I'm nervous, hon."

"Are you afraid the plane will crash?"

"I know it won't. I just—"

The stewardess came by and beamed down at Suzu the way people usually do. "Are we all settled in here?" she said. "Would you like some magazines?"

"I want to fly plane," Suzu said.

All of a sudden I realized she really thought she was going to drive the airplane! "You can't fly the plane," I said. "The pilot does that."

Then Suzu made a big fuss and began saying, "*I* fly plane!" She started to cry and everyone was looking over at us and the stewardess was looking worried. Then she went away and came back and said, "Well, the pilot said he'd be glad to have you come and watch him for a little while, Suzu. Then you can learn how."

Suzu jumped right up. "I fly plane?"

"Well, if you want to learn to fly, you'll have to take lessons. There's something called a license. Would you like to come too?" she said to me.

I guess I should've said Yes, but Suzu had been making such a fuss I almost didn't want people to know she was my sister. So I stayed and sat next to Mom who was blowing big pink bubbles with her bubble gum. "How come *your* bubbles are so big?" I said.

"Hmm?" Mom said. "Oh, practice, I guess."

"Are you still nervous?"

"Sort of."

But once we got up in the air, it was better. Suzu kept running around and making the stewardess bring her special things like bags of goldfish crackers.

"That's a mighty cute little sister you have," a man said to me when I got up to go to the bathroom.

"Yes, she's pretty cute," I said. "She's adopted. She comes from Vietnam."

"She reminds me of my granddaughter, Essie," he said. "Real little devil of a girl, but winds you around her finger in no time flat."

What's Your Bag?

We've been in California a week already. Even though we're staying at this house that belongs to these friends of Dad and Peggy, we visit Dad and Peggy a lot. I love their house. When I grow up, I want to live in a dome too. Sometimes I sleep over. There's a big sign on the room where I sleep that says "What's Your Bag?" And inside the room is one huge mattress. It covers the whole floor of the room and lined up on it are different colored sleeping bags. I can sleep in whichever one I want. That's all there is in the room except for big posters and pictures. Dad and Peggy sleep in something like a bunk bed only it's called a loft. Under it is a desk and they let me sit there and type.

All Mom does all day is lie around in the sun.

"I thought you never got tan so you said it wasn't worth the bother," I told her.

"I don't think I ever really *devoted* myself to being lazy before," she said.

She's really brown and at night she dresses up in these pretty dresses with flowers on them. I almost don't recognize her because at home Mom usually wears slacks. Suzu doesn't wear anything. She says that since Jacob doesn't, she doesn't have to. She's brown all over, even her behind.

One interesting thing I never saw before is that Peggy is nursing Jacob. She just walks around with him sucking at her breasts. Her breasts are really big, not like Mom's. She even cooks and does things with him sucking onto her. Once at lunch Suzu said, "Put milk on pudding," to Peggy. Peggy started to pour it from the carton and Suzu said, "Want it from there," meaning Peggy's breast. So Peggy squeezed a shot into Suzu's pudding. "I like breasts," Suzu said.

During the day Peggy goes away to her job. She leaves Jacob with a babysitter named Keshia. Jacob seems like a good baby, except he has this pink spot on his face. "It's a strawberry mark," Peggy told us.

"He eats strawberries?" Suzu said.

"No! That's just an expression," I said.

"I touch?" she asked Peggy.

"Sure."

Suzu poked at the place. Jacob didn't seem to mind. He doesn't seem to mind much. He just lies there and sucks his toes and smiles. Even when a fly is on his face, he just lies there and doesn't mind.

"I don't know where I got this placid baby," Peggy said to Mom. It was Saturday and we had come over at five, which is when Peggy gets home from work. "I mean, according to my mother *I* never sat still long enough for her to lay her hands on me. He is just so good-natured, I don't believe it."

"Bernie was exactly the same way," Mom said. She was drinking this thing Peggy makes in her blender from papayas, lemon, and bananas. Only she adds rum and that wrecks it. "I never knew what people meant when they said they had all that trouble with babies the first year. And the terrible twos—she never had *one* tantrum. I used to worry something was the matter with her, she seemed so calm."

"It must be Fumio," Peggy said.

"It has to be," said Mom. "Of course, now Bernie is moody as all get-out at times, so I certainly don't worry about her anymore."

"I am *not* moody as all get-out," I said.

"Bernie, I thought you were outside playing. Will you look at her, pale as a ghost and the rest of us so brown!"

"I like to be indoors."

"Don't you love it out here?" Peggy said. "I wish you'd all move out here. Fumio would just love it. He misses Bernie so much."

"It *is* a great place," Mom said.

"You look just fantastic, Becka," Peggy said. "When you first came out here, you were so tired looking."

"Well, it's been a rough year," Mom said.

"You know, what I love here is that you can be outdoors all year round," Peggy said. "It almost never rains. You just feel so much better physically."

I went outside. Jacob was lying on a towel in this pen he has. I saw Suzu go over and take his bottle of juice away. He yelled.

"What are you doing?" I said.

"Nothing," she said.

I went over. "Bottles are for babies. You're too big for them."

She frowned.

"Put it back," I said. "If they hear him yelling, they'll come out."

"Don't like baby," Suzu said. "Baby yucky. Put baby in beezlenut oil."

"Oh, come on. It's not even our baby. You're not supposed to be jealous of him."

"Baby bit me," Suzu said.

"Well, don't put your finger in his mouth. What do you expect him to do?" I took the bottle and put it back in the pen. Jacob was just lying there making these mad sounds.

When I got back, Suzu was sitting down, her legs apart. "Sand in 'gina," she said crossly.

"Well, if you wore clothes once in a while, that wouldn't happen."

"Itchy," she said.

"Well, let's go in the pool."

Dad and Peggy have this great pool shaped like a baseball mitt. There's a shallow part where we have to stay unless a grown-up is around. Suzu isn't allowed to go in unless I'm there. The funny thing is, Suzu can swim really well. She just went in and started swimming, without even knowing how. One time she swam all the way down to the deep end. I didn't tell her that was good because I didn't want her to get vain.

Dad came late, and he and Mom and Peggy sat outside to eat. He grilled something on this Japanese stove they have. It was some kind of fish. They're vegetarians, except for fish.

I guess I feel a little bit jealous of the baby too. Of course, I'm too old for that and I would never steal his bottle. But sometimes I imagine that he drowns or something like that. It's hard to see why grown-ups think babies are so great.

"Where's that fine, strapping lad?" Dad said. He tossed Jacob way up in the air and Jacob laughed and laughed.

"Throw *me* up!" Suzu said.

"You're too heavy, honey," Mom said.

"No, I'm not," Suzu said. She is pretty heavy, though. She weighs almost forty pounds. I know because I put a penny in this machine for her.

After supper Mom and Suzu went home, but I

stayed to sleep over. As I was getting into my sleeping bag, Dad asked me if I'd like to come into the city with him on Monday. I said Yes.

Dad works in San Francisco in a big office building. San Francisco is like New York in some ways but with more hills. What's funny is that even though I know New York is supposed to be a big city, it doesn't seem big to me because I know it. Like in the summer, I feel I can walk down Fifth Avenue and wear shorts and sandals or anything, but the people who visit there look all dressed up.

Dad introduced me to some people at his office.

"So, this is Bernie, the famous writer!" one man said. "I'm glad to meet you."

Dad said he had showed them some of my stories.

"He never stops talking about you," one lady said.

Dad's office is big with a lot of books on one wall. "Someday I'll have your books up here, Bern," he said, sitting down in his chair. He showed me the models for some houses he was building. One was a school and another was a library. I can see it would be interesting to build houses for people, but I don't think I'd want to do it.

We walked someplace for lunch and Dad pointed things out to me. Once he stopped and went into a store to buy a toy for Jacob Nguyen.

It was a wooden fish puzzle that you shake back and forth. "Do you think he'll like it?" he said.

"Sure, I guess. Maybe, the thing is, Dad, could we get something for Suzu too? Because if you just bring home a present for Jacob, she might get jealous."

Dad looked surprised, but he said, "That's a nice idea. You better pick it, Bernie."

I chose a little dragon with a tail that moved.

"How about you, honey? Would you like anything?"

I really hadn't meant that I wanted something, but the store did have nice things so I ended up getting some origami paper. I can make animals for Suzu with it.

"So, what do you think of California?" Dad said. "Do you like it?"

I nodded. "Yes, it's nice." I kept thinking what if what Mom had said had happened, if Dad had kidnaped me or whatever the word was and I was living out here all the time. But the thing is, I don't think I would like that. First of all, I would miss New York and school and Jonah and all of that. But also, well, it just wouldn't be the same with Dad now that he's married and has a baby. I heard Peggy tell Mom she wants to have another baby next year. I know this sounds awful, but if Dad had a little girl, I would really be jealous, much more than I feel with Jacob. And he might, you can't tell. I know he still loves me, it's not that, but it wouldn't be the same. Like I can tell he doesn't really love Suzu, the way he forgets about her. Because she's not his child. She's not part of his family. Maybe if Mom died or something and Suzu and me had to live with Dad and Peggy, then it would be different. But I don't want that to happen either.

"You look so serious, sweetheart," Dad said. "What're you thinking about?"

"You might get mad at me if I tell you," I said.

"I won't, I promise."

"Well, I think I wouldn't want to live out here all the time with you and Peggy."

"Oh, well, of course not," Dad said. "Your home is with Becka in New York. But I hope you'll visit a lot, now that you're old enough to travel by yourself. You might come to college out here."

College! That's about a thousand years away.

"What's happened with Gabe?" Dad asked me. "I'm scared to ask Becka for fear she'll bite my head off."

I laughed to think of Mom biting Dad's head off. "Do you promise to keep a secret?"

"Sure."

"Swear not to even tell Peggy."

Dad raised his hand. "I swear."

"I got this letter from Francesca."

"Francesca?"

"Gabe's daughter from his first marriage. You

remember, Dad. He was married to this prom queen who—"

"Oh, yes, I do recall."

"Well, in her letter Francesca said she and Gabe might be coming to live in New York. She said her mother was sick."

"Hmm, that's too bad—about her mother, that is. Does Becka know?"

"No. No one knows but me."

"Curious he wouldn't get in touch with her. He was a strange fellow, I guess."

"He didn't used to be in the beginning. Mom said after he lost his job he sort of freaked out. He didn't like the idea of living off her, he said."

Dad just shook his head. "Well, it's all over and done with. Someday Becka will find someone who can handle her."

"Why should she?" I looked at him. "She's O.K. the way she is."

He looked embarrassed. "For you, though—to have a father."

"I do have one. I have you."

He reached down and hugged me. "I have to admit it, now that he's gone—I was always a little jealous of Gabe, seeing you every day."

That's really funny. I never thought grown-ups could be jealous the way children are. "I never loved him, though, Dad. I just liked him a little bit."

Dad laughed. "That's good," he said.

At the end of the day Dad drove me back to

our house. I gave Suzu the dragon. She seemed to like it and kept wiggling its tail back and forth till the end part fell off. Mom said she would fix it.

Baby Weekend

"Bernie and Suzu and I just came up with a great idea," Mom said to Peggy the next day. "Why don't the two of you go off for the weekend and leave Jacob here with us? Just go and have a ball and forget you ever heard the word baby."

At first Peggy kept saying No, they couldn't, and it wasn't fair to us. Mom said, "Don't be silly. We know all about babies. We're experts."

I don't know why she said that. I don't see how we're such experts! But anyway, finally Dad and Peggy said it was really sweet of us and they thought they would.

"You don't remember about babies," I said after they left.

"Oh, it's a cinch. He's a little lamb, aren't you, fat old Jacob Nguyen?"

"You said you purposely adopted Suzu when she wasn't a baby because babies bugged you."

"Bernie, do you have to remember every word that was ever said? One weekend with a baby will be fun! It's not like it's a year!"

But that afternoon Jacob woke up and seemed very mad when Mom tried to give him the bottle. He tried to spit it out and waved his hands around and turned red. You could tell he was angry.

"You put milk in your breast," Suzu said to Mom.

"You can't *put* milk in it," I said. "It's either there or it's not."

"He's mad," Suzu said, watching the baby screaming. "He doesn't like us."

"He likes us," Mom said. "He just isn't used to us yet."

"What if he doesn't get used to us all weekend? What if he starves to death? Would they put us in jail?" I said.

"Bern, could you tamp down that wonderful active imagination of yours? Babies never starve. They're too smart for that."

"Some of them do. In India and places like that."

"That's because there's no food."

"I'm going to go and type," I said.

"You do that," Mom said. "Suzu and I will figure out how to deal with this marvelous specimen here."

I decided to do just a couple more recipes for

my cookbook. The trouble is, the rest of it is back home, but I remember it. I'll just do a few little snacks, nothing too fancy. I had lots of drinks planned for the Beverages section, but all of a sudden Suzu came running in saying, "It's raining!"

Big deal! I've seen plenty of rain before. What's so great about rain? But this rain was odd. It was just pouring straight down, with no thunder or lightning or anything.

I went into the kitchen. "Did he drink?" I said to Mom.

"Bernie, that baby is a beast! Who said babies were so great? Who convinced me to take on this beast for a whole weekend?"

"No one convinced you," I said. "You just did it."

"No! I'm not that dumb. I refuse to believe it. I think you put a magic spell on me. Hey, I have a great idea!"

"What?"

"Let's wash our hair in the rain! It's great for your hair, rainwater. It makes it all silky. Quick, I'll get the shampoo." So we all ran outside in our bathing suits, except Suzu who was naked, of course, and we jumped around and whooped and soaped our hair and rinsed it off. It was so much fun!

Then we came inside. "You know, what this place needs is more rain," Mom said.

"And snow," I said.

"Right. What do they think they are, doing away with the seasons like that?"

"Jacob's up, Mom. I hear him."

"He can't be. He just spent two solid hours eating. He's supposed to sleep through the night."

"He cry," Suzu said happily. "Want to see baby cry."

"He must be hungry again," I said.

"Well, I'm hungry," Mom said. "I'm starved, in fact. Oh, go get him, Bern. If he's wet, pamper him, O.K.?"

Jacob didn't seem hungry really. He just sat in his infant seat and watched us have supper.

"Want to see baby cry," Suzu said, scowling.

"Please!" said Mom. "Be grateful for small favors."

Suddenly Jacob's face got all serious and he turned bright red. "Uh oh," Mom said. "He's mad again. Oh, no, I think he's just making a b.m."

"Not like b.m.?" said Suzu. "He mad."

"No, it's just a lot of work for him."

"Should I change him again?"

"Yes, I guess. He might get a rash."

It wasn't such a great weekend, but when Peggy and Dad came home, we said it had been great. "He's a darling," Mom said.

"I guess I should say I missed him every second," Peggy said, "but, in fact, we had a marvelous time. Hi, big guy! What's new?"

I wrote letters to Jonah and to Grandma. I told Grandma that if Sol was going to weave me a rug for my room, it should be red and blue and purple. When I was in the middle of writing, Mom came in. "Bern, I've been thinking. When we go home, why don't we try and fix up the study for you? I'll clear out all that junk and it'll be really nice. You and Suzu can still sleep together when you want to, but this can be a kind of retreat, sort of out of the way up there."

"I can put Sol's rug down next to the desk," I said, imagining it, "and——"

"What d'you mean?"

I turned red. "Oh, Grandma's friend, Sol. He weaves."

"He weaves, eh? Come on, Bern, spill the beans. You know something you're not telling."

"No, I don't. Anyway, you'll shoot her if you know."

"Uh oh. I better sit down for this."

"I promised not to tell."

"Out with it!"

"Do you promise not to shoot Grandma?"

"I promise."

"Do you promise not even to get mad at her? Or even to tell her I told you?"

"I do."

"Well, she——she's married to him."

"What?"

"He's a weaver."

"Sure, and I'm a candlestick maker and——"

"It's a hobby. He used to be a lawyer, only he

was coming into this store where Grandma works to buy some organic peanut butter and—"

"One thing led to another. Oh, wonderful!" Mom shrugged. "Look, why not? Am I such a big expert on love and marriage?"

"No," I said.

"Bernie!"

"You asked me."

Mom shook her head. "Bern, there's one thing you're going to have to learn: you were born knowing everything else, but you're going to have to learn how to lie."

"Mom?"

"Yes?"

"You're a big expert on love and marriage."

"Liar!"

Dad and Peggy said they were really sorry we were going and they hoped we would think over the idea of coming to live in California someday. Mom said Sure, it certainly was appealing, but I knew she didn't really mean it. "You come see *us* next time," she said. "We can put you up easily, can't we, Bern?"

I said we could.

Francesca

On the plane going home Suzu made a fuss again. She said the lady on the other plane said she could fly the plane herself on the way back. So all the stewardesses were running around trying to make her happy and giving her special magazines and straws.

When she was back there playing with them, I said to Mom, "Are you sorry we adopted Suzu?"

"No, why should I be sorry?"

"Well, you said to Peggy how much easier it would be without children."

"Hon, listen," Mom said. "Sometimes, of course I feel that way. Just like you sometimes feel life would be easier without me. But most of the time I feel that without the two of you life wouldn't be worth a hang. Having things easy isn't what it's all about."

"What *is* it all about?"

"When I find out, I'll let you know."

When we arrived in New York, it was one in the morning. That's the latest I ever stayed up in my whole life! Of course, I slept a little bit on the plane. Suzu was sound asleep so Mom had to carry her. "This is no baby," Mom said. "This is an elephant."

"She weighs forty pounds," I said.

"You better believe it," Mom said.

Finally we got this cab and he put our bags in and Mom told him our address. I felt so excited to be going home again! I kept picturing in my mind our house with all the stuff in it, my typewriter, the stove, everything. It may sound funny to say you can miss a typewriter, but you can. I yawned. "Mom?"

"Umm?" Mom looked sleepy too.

"It's funny, but I don't feel Dad and Peggy and Jacob are my family the way you and Suzu are."

"How come?"

"I don't know. I just don't."

"Do you think we're a good family?" Mom said, suddenly looking worried.

"Sure."

"No, I mean, it doesn't seem right, Bernie, to put you through all these changes. Sometimes I think if you really would be happier with Dad and Peggy, you should go out there to live. It would be a regular family and maybe you need that."

"I don't want to. I like our family."

"Do you really, honey?"

"When I go to college, maybe I'll go out there," I said sleepily.

We drove up in front of our house.

"Mom?"

Mom was paying the driver. "What?"

"There's a light on in our house."

"A light?"

"There—in the living room."

Mom looked at me. She looked scared.

"Do you think it's a robber?" I said.

The cab driver said, "Should I get the police?"

"No, no," Mom said. "I'll tell you what you can do. Bern, let the cab driver lift you up so you can see who's there, O.K.?"

The cab driver was kind of big and smelly, but he did lift me up. "It's Gabe," I said.

"Jesus Christ!" Mom said.

"Someone you know?" said the driver.

"In a manner of speaking," Mom said. "O.K., we can handle this." She paid him and he drove away.

Gabe was sitting in the living room, reading a book. When he saw us, he said, "Well, hi there! Welcome back!"

"Welcome back, my foot!" said Mom. She looked angry. She laid Suzu down on the couch.

"I will give you exactly ten minutes flat to get out of this house and not one minute more."

"Becka!" Gabe stood up. "You don't understand. Francesca is here."

"She is? Where is she?" I said. I felt really excited.

"She's sleeping in your room, Bernie."

I ran in. There was Francesca sitting up in my bed. "Hi, Bernie."

"Hi." She looked different from the time at the wedding. She was still tall with red hair, but she looked prettier. She was wearing this really pretty nightgown with lace on it. Reaching around, she found some glasses and put them on.

We went back into the living room. Mom was pointing to the door. "Out!" she said. She looked like a general. "Out, out, out of this house!"

"Becka, it's nearly two in the morning. Be sensible."

"My mother had a nervous breakdown," Francesca said, "and I'm living with Daddy now."

"Well, *I'm* going to have a nervous breakdown if I don't hear a very good explanation for all this," Mom said. "Have you been here the whole time we've been away?"

"Becka, will you—"

"This had better be a beaut," said Mom sniffing.

"Look, Francesca and I just got to the city last week," Gabe said. "We haven't had time to find a place yet. Naturally, this thing with Muriel came as a tremendous shock. I just thought we could stay here a few days."

"Listen, buster, you do not walk out of a house and walk back six months later without batting an eye. Why didn't you write and let me know where you were?"

"I'm sorry. I should have." Gabe looked over at me. "Can't we at least stay till morning?"

"Oh, Mom, let them!" I said. "Please!" I wanted so much to talk to Francesca.

"O.K., till morning. But that's *it*. Absolutely."

Francesca and I stayed up late talking. We talked quietly so Suzu wouldn't wake up. She said she was excited about coming to live in New York. "I hope you don't mind," she said. "I was in that room upstairs and I saw your notebooks. I love your stories." She smiled in this shy way. "I do drawings," she said. "I did some drawings to go with your stories."

"You did?" I could hardly wait to see them. "We could publish books together," I said.

"That's what I thought," she said. "I'm going to use a pseudonym, though. Francesca Fox. I like that better than Francesca Sobel."

I had never thought of that. "Maybe I should too," I said.

"You could be Bernadette Blossom."

"I don't like that. But I'll think some more. I'm really glad you came here."

"You're different from what I imagined," Francesca said.

"How?"

"Well, Daddy said he always thought you could see right through him. I thought you'd be scary."

I laughed.

"Goodnight, Bernie. Sweet dreams."

"Goodnight, Francesca. Do people call you that or do they call you Frannie?"

"Sometimes they call me Fran, but I like Francesca better."

"Sweet dreams, Francesca."

I slept till ten the next morning. When I woke up, Suzu was up playing and Francesca was just brushing her teeth. I went inside. I thought maybe Mom had let Gabe sleep in her bed after all, but he was in the living room sleeping on the couch. Finally Mom came out, dressed in one of her California flowered dresses. We all had breakfast. I made French toast.

"Want French toast to talk," Suzu said.

"She always does that," I told Francesca.

"She's so cute. Does she let you dress her up and stuff like that?"

"Uh *uh!*"

"Why did you get so beautiful in California?" Gabe said to Mom. "That's not playing fair, Becka."

Mom turned red and said, "Let's not get into *that* kind of thing."

"Are you still as grumpy and unrelenting as ever?"

"Worse," Mom said. "I've gotten *worse.*"

"Jesus, look at you! Your skin and everything."

"I'm much worse," Mom said warningly. "In fact, I'm a holy terror. You ask Bernie."

"She is," I said because I knew Mom wanted me to say that.

Francesca whispered, "Is your mother really a holy terror?"

"She's mean sometimes," I said, "but mostly she's pretty good."

After breakfast Gabe and Francesca went out to look at apartments. Mom looked at me.

"In the Brady Bunch," I said, "there's this man with three boys and he meets this woman with three girls and they get married."

"I think I'm going to throw up," Mom said.

"They have lots of fun together."

"I'll bet they do. Bern, look, we're a family, right? Just the three of us, perfectly good, fine family and Gabe and Francesca are a perfectly good, fine family. So let's quit all this Brady Bunch stuff, O.K.?"

"Don't you like Francesca, though? Isn't she beautiful?"

"I certainly don't think she's a beautiful girl, no, but she seems very sweet. I want to get to know her."

"If you have a nervous breakdown, would I go to live with Gabe and Francesca or Dad and Peggy?"

"I'm not going to have a nervous breakdown,"

Mom said, licking the syrup off her fingers. "I don't have the time."

"Well, you better not. Because I want to live right here in this house."

"That's exactly where you're going to live, Bernie. Right here in this house."

"Want house to talk," Suzu said.

"The house says, 'I'm very glad to have you back, folks. I missed you,'" Mom said.

"We missed you, house," I said. It's true. I did.

The Christmas Party

Mom did fix up the study for me. It makes a really great place to type. It's small, but it has curtains at the windows and a bean-bag chair in the corner. Francesca and I come up here a lot to talk. Of course, we play with Suzu too. It's funny. Francesca is an only child so she thinks Suzu is really cute and actually *wants* to play with her. She says when she's thirteen, she's going to ask Mom if she can be Suzu's babysitter.

Francesca and Gabe are living in an apartment in Greenwich Village on Morton Street. Gabe is teaching sculpture at this college down there. Francesca's room is really small, even smaller than mine, but she has a sleeping bag so sometimes I sleep over. She's really good at drawing! She can draw really hard things like telephones and pine trees. She knows about making things seem far away. You should see the drawings she did for "Mamie and the Hebrew War." They were great! Especially the one of Mamie hiding when the rough woman came along the road in her car. She made the rough woman look really mean, just the way she was supposed to be. I decided I won't have a pseudonym after all. I'll just be Bernadette Nakamura or B. C. Nakamura if I want to be more mysterious. Even if I get married, I'll never change my name.

Francesca says she misses her mother, but she likes living with Gabe. He seems different now— at least he doesn't yell anymore. I guess he's glad to have a job and all. Sometimes he takes us places like to the Planetarium or the movies. I like him much more than I used to when he was my stepfather. Of course, I'll never like him as much as Dad, but that's O.K. You can like a lot of people, but you can only love a few. That's what Grandma says.

Grandma and Sol Lieberman have come to stay with us for Christmas. Mom said she's not really mad at Grandma. We're giving a party on Christmas Eve and Gabe is coming and so is Jonah and his family. Francesca and I made a lot of decorations and we helped Mom bake tons of cookies and make a wine punch.

"How do you like the rug, sweetheart?" Sol asked me. He's a tall, thin man with very nice green eyes. I love his rug! I put it right near my desk in the study.

"It's beautiful," I said.

"Will you look at those colors!" Grandma said. "Sol just has this genius for color."

"Francesca is good at color too," I said, but Francesca turned away. She gets very shy if you say she's good at things.

About thirty people came to the party. It was pretty crowded. Jonah kissed me under the mistletoe. I didn't think we were up to that stage yet, but he said that you're supposed to and I shouldn't worry that it means I'm his girlfriend because he doesn't have a girlfriend and he never intends to. I said that was O.K.

Gabe came with his girlfriend. She had blond hair in a bun. She drank three glasses of punch.

"I guess we might get drunk," Francesca said as Jonah and I were sipping our punch.

"I don't want to throw up," Jonah said uneasily.

"Eat some cookies then," Francesca said. "We made them."

Jonah ate around ten cookies. Now that he's growing, he can eat a million cookies and no one can tell. "You're really a great cook, Bernie," he said. "If I ever do have a girlfriend, it will be you. I didn't mean I don't like girls or anything."

"I know," I said. "I'm not going to have a boyfriend either because I'm never getting married, but you're still my best friend who's a boy."

Mom had turned out all the lights in the room and put candles all around. There was a nice piney smell from the boughs of trees which we'd hung all over. Mom was wearing a long dark-red velvet dress and she had some white flowers in her hair. She put some music on the phonograph and we all began to dance. It was a dance where you danced in a circle, everyone holding hands, weaving around and around. I was between Grandma and Suzu. Grandma squeezed my hand. "Don't you love him?" she whispered.

I wasn't sure who she meant at first, but then I saw she was looking at Sol. I nodded.

"If you find the right person, there's nothing better than that," Grandma whispered. "Don't let your mother tell you anything different."

"Who's going to light the candle at the top of the tree?" Mom said.

"I want to," Suzu said.

Sol reached down and picked Suzu up around the waist. He held her up high and she lit the candle at the very top of the tree. Then she ran over and grabbed my hand.

ABOUT THE AUTHOR

NORMA KLEIN grew up in New York City and received a B.A. from Barnard College and an M.S. in Slavic languages from Columbia University. She has published numerous short stories, adult novels, and books for young readers, including *Hiding*, *Naomi in the Middle* and *Tomboy*, which are available in Archway Paperback editions. Ms. Klein lives in New York City with her husband and their two daughters.

GROWING UP...
You Can't Run Away
from It and
You Don't Have To!

___29982 HIDING $1.75
Norma Klein
*Kril, shy and withdrawn, copes by "hiding"—until she meets
Jonathan, who helps her come out of her shell. "Tremendous
appeal."*—West Coast Review of Books

___42062 FIND A STRANGER, SAY GOODBYE $1.95
Lois Lowry
*Natalie is haunted by a missing link in her life—the identity of
her real mother—so she sets out on a journey to find her. "A
beautifully crafted story which defines the characters with a
full range of feelings and emotions."*—Signal

___42449 THE CHEESE STANDS ALONE $1.95
Marjorie M. Prince
*Daisy takes a stand for independence as she begins to see
herself in sharper focus through the eyes of the intriguing man
who paints her portrait. "Absorbing."*   —Publishers Weekly

___42450 CLAUDIA, WHERE ARE YOU? $1.95
Hila Colman
*Claudia feels suffocated by her family, and runs away to New
York City to find some kind of meaning in her life. "...presents
a thought-provoking view of a current social problem."*
                                                —English Journal

___29945 LETTER PERFECT $1.50
Charles P. Crawford
*The story of three friends caught up in a blackmailing scheme.
"Hard-hitting portrait of teenagers in crisis."*
                                              —Publishers Weekly

___41304 THE RUNAWAY'S DIARY $1.75
Marilyn Harris
*Fifteen-year-old Cat is on the road—in search of herself.
"Believable and involving."* —A.L.A. Booklist

___41674 GROWING UP IN A HURRY $1.75
Winifred Madison
*Karen discovers she is pregnant and must make a painful
decision. "A hard-hitting and brilliantly written novel."*
                                              —Publishers Weekly

ARCHWAY PAPERBACKS from Pocket Books

The Hopes, the Fears, the Problems of the Young... Jeannette Eyerly Understands Them

___41675 HE'S MY BABY, NOW $1.95
Charles is an unwed father who wants to keep his baby—but Daisy plans to give the child up for adoption. "Charles...is so touching, funny and believable...that readers can't help rooting for him."—Library Journal

___43214 THE PHAEDRA COMPLEX $1.75
Laura knew her life would change when her mother remarried, but she didn't expect to fall in love—with her stepfather. "Fans of...Mrs. Eyerly will not be disappointed!"
—English Journal

___29914 RADIGAN CARES $1.50
Doug Radigan has never been involved in anything, until he meets Emily and gets caught up in a political campaign. "A first-rate addition to an important body of work....Radigan rings very true."—Des Moines Sunday Register

___56031 SEE DAVE RUN $1.75
Dave Hendry runs away in search of his father. "A realistic portrayal of one of today's teens that will have a sledgehammer impact on the reader....The author has written a superb, insightful sketch of her character."—Signal

If your bookseller does not have the titles you want, you may order them by sending the retail price (plus 50¢ postage and handling for each order—New York State and New York City residents please add appropriate sales tax) to: POCKET BOOKS, Dept. AJE, 1230 Avenue of the Americas, New York, N.Y. 10020. Send check or money order—no cash or C.O.D.s—and be sure to include your name and address. Allow up to six weeks for delivery.

156

ARCHWAY PAPERBACKS from Pocket Books